'My
Story

Young
Nanny

Frances Mary Hendry

SCHOLASTIC

While the events described and some of the characters in this book may
be based on actual historical events and real people, Lily Hicks
is a fictional character, created by the author, and her diary
is a work of fiction.

Scholastic Children's Books
Euston House, 24 Eversholt Street,
London, NW1 1DB, UK
A division of Scholastic Ltd
London ~ New York ~ Toronto ~ Sydney ~ Auckland
Mexico City ~ New Delhi ~ Hong Kong

First published in the UK by Scholastic Ltd, 2001
This edition published 2010

Text copyright © Frances Mary Hendry, 2001
(as *My Story: The Crystal Palace*)
Cover image copyright © Richard Jones, 2010

ISBN 978 1407 11204 6

All rights reserved
Printed and bound by CPI Bookmarque, Croydon CR0 4TD

2 4 6 8 10 9 7 5 3

The right of Frances Mary Hendry to be identified as the author of this work
has been asserted by her in accordance with the Copyright, Designs
and Patents Act, 1988.

London, England
1850

Saturday, 8th June 1850
17 Charles Street, London

I, Lily Hicks, housemaid of Mr and Mrs Joseph Paxton do solemnly swear as every word I set down in this book shall be true.

Master hired this house for his cousin Mrs Judith McKenzie and her children and her husband, Major Jonathan McKenzie, as was wounded bad fighting in India. Thoughtful as always he asked me if I wanted to come here from Barbrook, his big house on the Duke of Devonshire's estate at Chatsworth, just while the Major and his wife are in England, so as to be near my mam as lives in Rotherhythe now. I was happy to oblige. Robert as was footman is made butler here, and I have to call him Mr Bibbings now. And we shall keep a bedroom and study for Master when he comes to London on business.

When I am trained proper, right up to 1st parlour-maid, Master says as he will speak to the Duke as he is a friend and patron as well as his 1st employer, or to his nephew, Lord Grafton, to get me a post as under-housekeeper in one of His Grace's grand houses. Some day I shall be Housekeeper at

Chatsworth itself, with a black lace apron and a bedroom and parlour of my own. So I am grateful, I do not want to upset him and Madam. They is the kindest anyone could hope for.

But I cannot let Mr Edgar McKenzie get any of us turned off neither, out of sheer badness. So this book shall tell all the things he done since he come from India. Not to get him into trouble, but to keep us out.

We had the house all ready on 3rd June when the McKenzies arrived. Cook hired, Mrs Smith that is, and Mary Jekyll as parlourmaid as I am not proper trained to wait at table, and Hannah the slavey and Billy the boots in the kitchen, and all cleaned and furnished and coals in – Master organizes everything ever so well – and even dinner in the oven, as a telegram had come saying as when they was coming. But they was all too fagged to eat. I carried Mr Edgar in myself and undressed him and put him to bed while Mr Bibbings helped the Major and Mary helped Mrs McKenzie and her daughter Miss Laura.

Next day Major stayed in bed. Mary and me was helping with unpacking. Mr Edgar come exploring downstairs. Cook was out to row the butcher that his mutton was not hung proper. Mr Bibbings was in the cellar racking 20 doz of claret. So Mr Edgar just found Hannah chopping veal for the Major's dinner, and Billy filling the lamps for downstairs, gas lighting being only in the Family and public rooms. He jeered at Hannah's red birthmark on her face till she cried.

He is 10, should know better, but gentry doesn't care nothing for servants' feelings – doesn't think we has none, I think.

Then he demanded cake and a cup of tea. Billy says as him and Hannah was not let touch the cake tins nor the tea-caddy, not even the servants' one with dried leaves from upstairs to use again, and besides they was stinky with whale oil and meat. Mr Edgar kicked him and shouted heathen words, he still has the bruise on his leg, Billy I mean. Mr Bibbings come up, hearing the din. Mr Edgar says as Billy had been rude and cheeky, when it was him, and Billy got rowed.

Next morning (Wednesday 5th) Mr Edgar come out of his bedroom while I was brushing the stair, and kicked the dustpan accidental, and then deliberate so it scattered dust through the banisters, and run back giggling. I was working from the top down, of course, so I hadn't done the hall yet. But he didn't know that, it could have give me lots more work.

Thursday 6th, Mrs Foley come visiting, a friend of Madam. Mary says as when she took in the tea-tray, Mrs McKenzie was complaining how careless and dirty Indian servants is, and always cheating you when you can't understand them, and stealing. Mrs Foley says as how English servants can be like that too. So she asks Mary, Isn't that right? And Mary says, Yes, Madam, but we are all careful and honest here. And the ladies laughed. But Mr Edgar looked ever so evil, Mary says.

So yesterday, Mary was called to the parlour over a Coalport figurine. Mr Edgar says as it was broke when he went in, but it was not. Mrs McKenzie has fined Mary 10/- – that is 2 weeks' wages – to pay for it, and warned her next time she is out. She is mad (Mary) and talking about leaving. Mr B says, Wait until I speak to Mr Paxton, he will see you right. So Mary will stay on for a while and see.

Then at servants' dinner last night, after saying grace Mr Bibbings stood up at the head of the table and says as young gentry has high spirits, as him and me knows from the Paxton children back home at Barbrook. Too right we does, in spite of Madam being so strict, but we has to put up with it. But breaking things as we are blamed for is too much. So, Mr Bibbings says as I should keep this record, to protect all of us, because I am best at reading and writing, as Master paid for me to go to school proper for 5 years. He will not row me if he sees me writing instead of working.

So while I am writing, I shall get off work, I think I'll take my time and write all the news. A good lark, even though my hand is sore with writing just this much.

Sunday, 9th June

Master called in to greet his cousin. He was racing round as usual, at the House of Commons, and then going to Wales to see his friend Mr Brunel's Britannia Bridge being floated into place, and then off to Derby to Midland Railway meetings as he is a Director of. But he stopped to ask if I was happy here. I says, Yes, Sir. Then Mr Bibbings took in the decanters, and says as Master was telling the Major as when he is fit to get out, Hyde Park is not far and a good place to stroll. He had been in there measuring up. What for? I says, and Mr B says, Master is going to offer a design for the new Hall for the Great Exhibition of the Industry of All Nations as Prince Albert is having so much trouble with. Too late, ain't it? Cook says. All the plans was to be in last week. But I says, if anybody can do it Master can, he is a wonder for work.

Mr Bibbings spoke to Master about Mr E, but he does not know what Master can do because Mrs McKenzie is his cousin, and expecting another baby at Christmas, as well as nursing the Major, so the Master will not want to upset her. 6 of Mrs McKenzie's children has died already in India of heat

7

and a snake and cholera, and her and Miss Laura near died too. We did not know this, though they all looks skinny and yellow.

Monday, 10th June

Mr E come up behind me and pinched my arm real sore.

Tuesday, 11th June

Mr E did nothing bad as we know of.

Wednesday, 12th June

Mr E banged the dinner gong early, upset everybody. But just naughtiness.

Friday, 14th June

Mr Edgar was in the kitchen for some cake, and shoved Hannah so she dropped a bowl of eggs. He laughed.

Sunday, 16th June

Mr Edgar tripped Mary in the hall while she was carrying out the tea-tray. Nothing broke because Mary got the cups to fall on the carpet, not the wood surround, but the sugar and slops went everywhere. He giggled when his mama run out at the clatter and rowed Mary. She is fit to spit teeth (Mary).

Mrs McKenzie is very sicky with the baby coming, and fratchy, always complaining and fussy and wanting little things done for her. She is used to lots of Indian servants, Mr B says, and never lifts a finger. They treats Mr E like a little god, and that is why he is so spoiled. But I feel sorry for her. Can't be easy living with nobody as speaks English, and snakes and crawlies everywhere, and you can't go out for the sun, and you fall sick and sweat all the time and get dreadful prickly rashes, (Mrs McK has scars all over, Mary says, just with scratching, she seen them when she was helping her dress) and your children die unless you send them away to England or take them up into the mountains in summer (as Mr B says) and lose your husband for 6 months every year. Nothing wrong with that, Cook says! But she has never been married, even though she is Mrs Smith. She has no time for men. Not like Mary.

Major was wounded in the belly and lucky to live. He is too ill and tired from the voyage for me to tell what he is like yet. Short and skinny, more hair in his moustache nor his head, sits in a chair in his dressing gown all day. Seems not to want to give bother.

Thursday, 20th June

Master come up to London today with plans for the new hall. We knew he could do it! Mary was serving tea (Mrs McK asks her to pour, her hands is not steady) so she heard it all (Mary I mean). Master says he sketched out the plan on his blotting paper during a Railway Tribunal hearing against a pointsman. Mrs McK says, Did no one complain?

Master says, Not the pointsman, he was fined 5/- and it should have been 10/-! Then he (Master I mean) went home and worked all night and all week to draw out his plan proper. He says his young men in the office was very good, and Mr Barlow, I think it was, as is an engineer from the Midland Railway.

The Major says, Does Mrs Paxton not object? But Master says, Sarah? No, she's used to it. (As is true, Master is often away days and days at meetings all over the country from 5 in the morning till after midnight, he is a terror for work, like when he first come to work for the Duke at 4 in the morning and nobody about, so he climbed the wall and when the gardeners come to work at 6 he had all their jobs planned out for them already! And in his office all hours when he is home.) He says on the train up he met his friend Mr Stephenson the engineer (son of the Stephenson who built the Steam Engine) as is on the Royal Commission planning the Exhibition, and he (Mr S) thinks the plan is wonderful, and though he thinks it is too late he will do what he can.

Lord Granville called. They rang for The Times, but Miss Laura had cut it up to make strips of dancing dolls to amuse Mr Edgar. Mr Bibbings sent Billy scudding to buy another. When Mary went in for the tea-tray Lord Granville told her, Take away that slop! We want brandy! She near dropped the tray again, that excited with being spoken to by a real live Lord. Mr B took in the tray with decanters of brandy and Madeira for Mrs McK, and he says as Lord Granville poured out glasses for them all with his own hand, and made a toast to Master. We'll see you Sir Joseph Paxton yet! he says.

Just as Mr B opened the door to leave, Mr E banged the dinner gong again. His Lordship jumped and spilled brandy all down his coat, but he just laughs, and says, A libation to the gods! (Mr B says it means a gift of wine, as is a heathen custom.) A sure sign of success! But the Major scolded Mr E after.

We think what they wanted to see in The Times was a piece about the Exhibition. Architects all over the world has put in plans, but they all cost too dear, so the Building Committee has made their own. But The Times says as how their building is very ugly and should not be allowed. So we all hope Master's plan will be accepted instead.

Miss L and Mr E has been told to use yesterday's newspapers for playing.

Mr B spoke again to the Master, and Mary does not have to pay for the broken figurine. So Mary is happy, and Master is looking sideways at Mr Edgar.

Friday, 21st June

Mr E quiet but sulky.

Found a pretty painting of roses under Miss Laura's bed,

and asked if I might make so bold as to keep it. And she says as she will paint me a better one, of a lily as is my name. She is very pleasant, pretty manners and no stinking pride, and cleverer nor anybody except the Master and Mistress, I am sure. Her skin is yellowish, like her mama's, with being sick and the sun in India. She has to keep wrapped up because she feels cold, though it is ever so nice out.

Master arrived to spend the night before going to the Royal Commission tomorrow. We are all excited for him.

Saturday, 22nd June

This morning Lord Granville took Master in his own carriage to speak to the Commission, with Queen Victoria and Prince Albert.

Major has ordered the Illustrated London News, and the Commission's own plan is printed in it. 17 million bricks, and cost £300,000 – and all to come down after 6 months! Ridiculous, Cook says, and we all agree.

Master come back this afternoon very excited under his usual calm. Queen and Prince Albert like his plan. So Master went down the Mall to the London office of Fox & Henderson as makes the ironwork for his glass houses and knows what he wants, and luckily Mr Fox himself was there, not up in Birmingham, and they agreed to telegraph Mr Chance as makes glass for them – he has the biggest glass factory in the country, near Mr Fox's ironworks in Birmingham so they can work together easy – to come to Town on Monday and make plans.

This evening Master was called to the Palace for a long talk with Prince Albert.

We cannot think about anything else, we are that excited, even Mr E. But he has not been bad today.

Monday, 24th June

Mrs McK hid a half-sovereign under the carpet in the dining-room, to check if I was thorough and honest, they all does it. But I saw Mr E spying at the door out of the corner of my eye, and when I took it from my apron pocket and handed it to her he was there and looked disappointed, and she was surprised. He must have told her as I was stealing it. So she says I can keep it, for honesty, as is not normal. Will get 3 yards of twill for a new Sunday skirt. So he done me a good turn, ha ha.

My afternoon off tomorrow. Going to visit Mam, first time

since she come to London. She says it is not as grand as the cottage at Chatsworth, in Edensor Village as Master designed for the Duke of Devonshire, with blue and white china and a neat garden and a pig.

Tuesday, 25th June

The Times says the Exhibition should not be in Hyde Park, but in Battersea to avoid annoyance to the genteel residents of Knightsbridge. Says it is insanity, and an outrage, and the whole area will be turned into a bivouac for vagabonds (that's a camp for tramps, Mr B says). They is always against Prince Albert, anything he says is wrong. But I like him, he is handsome.

Later

Have to write this down, I am that upset. Wrote Mam last week to meet me on Paradise Lane, as sounded nice. But she was not there, and it was rough, but I asked a roast-chestnut man,

15

and found Haggs Alley at last. Stinking filthy slum, pigs rooting in gutters, no windows only shutters and sacks. Glad I had on my old clothes, not my Sunday best, or the half-starved bare-foot ragabags scratching their bums at all the corners would have mugged me. Found Mam at last, up 4 floors all dark and grimy, attic with a cracked skylight, all of them in 1 room, Mam and Jake and Betsy and Ben and little Davy, and leaks and cracks and black mould everywhere.

Good to see Mam again, but she was that ashamed, and her always so proud of her nice cottage, till Dad lost it all. I was cursing him, but Mam says, Lily, he was provoked. It's not poor folk's place to get provoked by their betters, I says, and getting himself sacked and losing his house. He did his best after, Mam says, working in the slaughterhouse with pay and good pickings, till the lung rot took him last year. But London is so dear, 2/- a week rent and bread at 8½d a loaf, even with them all working all hours making buttons and Mam sewing gloves they can just barely scrape by.

Give Mam the half-sovereign.

Come back to No 17 right low, and Mr E sniggers, Your face is tripping you, Lily, is something wrong? Nasty little weasel.

Wednesday, 26th June

Mr E run to his mama crying, saying as Ratter bit him. Billy says as he (Mr E) was teasing Ratter and pulling Ratter's tail, though how I do not know, it was only half an inch long. Mrs McKenzie says as Ratter must be drowned at once. Mr Bibbings says as how Ratter was a good terrier and useful, but he had to do as he was told. Billy cried all night, Ratter was his dog, I thought as it was a snappy little beast, but Billy loved it. We think that is why Mr E made such a fuss, just to hurt Billy. Little d***l.

Saturday, 29th June

Master come in this afternoon with Lord Grafton and Mr Cole as started the idea for the Exhibition, and another gent as I don't know, all very merry, and Major and Mrs McKenzie come out into the hall at the laughter and Lord Grafton told them as Prime Minister as was, Sir Robert Peel has spoke for the Master's plan in Parliament, and Prince Albert has praised it to the Royal Commission, and Fox & Henderson will put in a tender for it and pay Master £2,500 if it is accepted!

We was all listening at the green baize door to the servants' hall, and we cheered, and Master called us out. Thought we was in trouble for earwigging, but Mr Bibbings spoke up brave, We are all proud and glad of the honour and the recognition of your skill and craftsmanship, Sir, as is no more nor your due. Never thought he had it in him, Mr B I mean, he is that shy. But Miss Laura clapped, and Master told Mr B to share a bottle of port among us all. Makes you tiddly quick, even half a glass what I got.

Mr Edgar was jumping about, and Miss L told him to be quiet, and he pushed her so hard she fell over a stool. So he got scolded, all sulky again. He sat on Master's new tall hat as cost 19/-, near 3 months of my wages, and dented it so bad Mr B says it will never come right. Says it was an accident, but I wonder.

Sunday, 30th June

Yesterday Sir Robert Peel was thrown from his horse.

Wednesday, 3rd July

Sir Robert Peel died last night.

Commission has turned down Master's plan, they will build their own. Sneering at Master, saying he ain't trained, not an architect, not even an engineer, just a gardener. We are all furious. Miss L was near crying. Mr E was sniggering in corners.

Thursday, 4th July

House of Commons says the best memorial for Sir Robert would be the thing as he supported, Master's plan for the Exhibition Hall. But it is up to the Commission. Mrs McK says, I just wish they'd decide one way or the other, and get it over, but the Major says, If they take on Joseph's idea, my dear, it will just be the start of it.

Saturday, 6th July

Master's plan printed in the Illustrated London News, far better nor the other, a big glass-house like the Stove House at Chatsworth and the new glass-house for the Victoria Regia lily as keeps on growing and needing a bigger house, the one he sat Miss Annie (as was 7) on its leaf and it held her. Much cheaper, and easy to break down and clear away after. Even Mr E impressed.

Sunday, 7th July

Woke up at 5 with toothache and went down to the kitchen for a clove. Billy was lighting fires for Hannah to make servants' breakfast. First time I had a chance to talk to them alone, without Cook or Mr B as makes them nervous.

Hannah does not want to stay a slavey, wants to be a cook. Her dad is a coal whipper, shovelling coal into baskets to haul up out of barges, 20 feet up sometimes, 200 tons a day they can shift, a gang of 9 men, she says, and 15/- each in just 5 days if there is a rush, but only when the barges comes in, not steady work, and hard, and dangerous as baskets holds near 200 lb and can split or ropes break any second. Her mam's dead.

Billy says as he was 11th in the family, half-starved, his mam wanted to sell him to a sweep but he run away and begged till Cook took him in here. No wonder Cook complains she can't keep him fed.

When she was 6 Hannah went to work in a pin factory, picking out pins all jumbled in a bin and setting them neat in papers to sell. Pricked like h**l, she says, her fingers was all bleeding. Her little sister Vera looked after the baby. But when Vera was 6, and could work and earn enough to pay a baby-minder 6d a week, she left (Hannah I mean) and come here. It is hard and less money and her fingers gets red raw from scrubbing pots, not from pins, but she is fed and with a proper bed and uniform and she has the chance to get on.

Told her I'd teach her to read and write, so she can read cookery books and write shopping lists. She near cried with thankfulness and says as she will love me for ever. Silly sausage, I says.

Billy says as he does not want to learn, only sissies can read. I think he is scared he is too stupid to learn so he will not try. Silly Billy, I says, and he got peeved so I clipped his ear.

21

Tuesday, 9th July

Mr E dirtied his trousers today, rubbing his shoes on them, and says as Billy should have cleaned them better, the shoes I mean. Billy got rowed. White trousers on boys is stupid, but the gentry does not have to wash their own clothes.

Friday, 12th July

Master has ordered his breakfast 2 hours early from now on. Cook is peeved, she has 4 breakfasts to make now, and Mr E a fussy eater. She says £8 a year is not enough, she is going to look for another place. I says as I could make Master's breakfast, but she just sniffed, Don't put yourself forward, Lily, haven't you enough to do? So I don't think she will go. But now Hannah has to make Cook tea at 4 as well as the servants' breakfast at 7, so the stove fire has to be built up by half 3. Lucky the McK's are early bedders – we wouldn't never get no sleep if they had parties till midnight like some does.

Tuesday, 16th July

Master in London most days now to meet people. Mr B says as the tenders has been accepted for the Hall. It is to be built by January, only 5 months, and to be opened on May Day. And nothing done yet!

They was talking about it at dinner, Mr B says, and Master says the Commissioners hasn't signed the contract yet but Mr Fox will go ahead and start the work at his own risk. Mr E (hopeful of mischief) asks, If it isn't signed, Uncle Joseph, will you have to pay for it all? Master says very firm, No, Edgar, Lord Granville says it's sure to go through, Fox will be paid in the end and I am not liable in any case.

He'll look a fool, though, if it ain't done, Cook says. It will be, I says, if anybody can do it in the time Master can. You don't know him, I says, he has designed gardens and parks and fountains and big stove houses all over, ever since he started working for His Grace of Devonshire before I was born, and got them built faster nor you'd believe. He can really make things work. And people! And Cook laughed, remembering how we worked to get the house ready, and nodded.

Some big elm trees are growing on the ground where the Hall is to be built, and people protested. Don't cut them down, they says, for a building as is only going to be there for 6 months! So Master changed his design to keep them happy. It was going to be a long hall in 3 storeys, and now he is going to put a cross-passage called a transept arching high over where the trees are. He says it will give the hall better proportions anyway. He grows trees inside the Stove House at Chatsworth, and moves them about, even one as weighed 20 ton, but I never heard of building over a tree.

Saturday, 20th July

Miss Laura heard me singing while I was dusting, a Sunday School hymn about children as mocked the Prophet Elisha. She did not scold me, but sat on the stair and nodded me to go on. But at the last verse, God quickly stopt their wicked breath, And sent 2 raging bears, That tore them limb from limb to death, With blood and groans and tears, Miss L begun laughing! She says, all giggly, I thought God loved children, Lily! He punishes them as He loves, I says sternly, till they repent of their sins. She just giggled again, Those children couldn't repent, not when they were in shreds, she says.

24

I didn't know where to look for shame for her, and she is 13, just a year younger nor me, she should know better.

But she give me my painting. Lovely big yellow lily with curling petals, like my fair hair, she says. It will not stay under my cap not if I try ever so.

Asked me about the servants, and I told her about helping Hannah. She (Miss L) says as there is some easy books in the schoolroom where her and Mr E studies in the mornings with her mama, and I can borrow them for Hannah. She is truly kind and I pray God will pardon her childish mocking.

Told her about writing a journal, but I was feared for my spelling. She will help me with it. She says, Will you come tomorrow? and I says, Not on a Sunday, Miss! But she says it will be a Sunday School. So I suppose it will be all right.

Sunday, 21st July

Miss L wrote me out words as I was getting wrong. So went back over this and put the words right from Miss L's list, and will do over and over as I learn more.

Miss L says, Can I come and visit with you next time you go home? No, Miss! I tells her straight, Your mama would be shocked, and your papa, and quite right, a genteel young lady like you don't want to come round the docks, it is dirty and rough with rats and that all over.

Mr E seems to have calmed down a bit. He is noisy, always clattering about and laughs like a donkey hee-haws, but he has not done nothing too wicked this month, only jeering at Hannah in the kitchen, but she keeps turned away, and Cook told her it was just bad manners. But I think it is nastiness.

Tuesday, 23rd July

What a to-do! My day off. Miss L was waiting for me in the street and says, I'm going home with you! Look, I'm wearing my plainest clothes so nobody will notice me! Her plainest maybe, but better nor anything round Mam's way. No, Miss, I says, but she just laughs. But I run both ways, I says, faster nor the horse buses, special if there is a lot of traffic, and even so I'll only get home for an hour or so, I says. I can run too, she says, and I'm coming, you can't stop me following you! So I give her my shawl to hide her fur collar, and put her fancy bonnet and gloves in my basket, and she come with me. She cannot run as fast as me, so could only stay half an hour. Betsy and Ben and Davy was very quiet and shy, but Cook had give me Saturday's left-over goose pie and a bit of cake, that cheered them up.

Mam was dreadful upset that a young lady should see the room, couldn't bring herself to say nothing at first. Miss L admired the buttons the children was sewing, when she got over panting, and tried her hand at it but the thread went all into knots, and they all laughed. It is not right to laugh at ladies, I told them, and she done better nor you done first time. And Miss L laughed too. That made Mam relax.

She (Miss L) was surprised as 5 of them lived all together with just the 1 straw mattress. Mam says, It is fine and light for work with the skylight, nor we don't need a fire even in winter, scarcely, with the heat coming up from the bakehouse in the cellar. (Not true, it is cold and damp, but she did not want to worry Miss L.) Ben has been took on to deliver for Bakey Hancock, he can get broken pies and that, and he will be a baker some day, so he is going up in the world like Lily, she says. But Jake has a nasty cough with the sawdust of cutting veneers. It is worrying her or she would not have said it.

Coming back, Miss L was interested in the stalls along Paradise Road, the spicers with their brown skins like in India. She could speak a few words to them in heathen as made them grin and bow. And a Chinaman bowed too, baggy trousers and button hat and long pigtail, I couldn't help staring. A man said he was Hee Sing, captain of a scruffy little ship in the docks. Who sing? I says. Hee Sing, says Miss L, and we giggled, but only when the Chinaman was away.

Miss L bought some roast chestnuts, and admired Mr Brice's glass dolls' eyes from France as he sells, and paid Dr Dominy a penny to see his bottled babies, them as is born dead and mis-shaped, preserved in formalin in big jars. Could not stop her, I thought as she would be sick but she loved them, special the one with 2 heads.

And when I says, Look, Miss, we're late, I'll get in ever such trouble! she stopped a hansom cab, fast 2-wheeler hackney, first time ever for me. Very awkward climbing in the front over the shafts, the iron step is small and wobbly and the apron door flaps. Don't know how the driver perched so high behind can control the horse. But Miss L told him, Hurry, whip up! and he did, right across town at a trot, and a canter if the road was clear. I hung on tight to the strap, bumpy over the cobbles, but fast. 2/6! All cabbies is d***ls for overcharging.

Late anyway. Run down the stair to the servants' door in the basement, but Mr B saw me when he opened the front door for Miss L. When he come down Cook was rowing me, and he did as well for getting too friendly with the Family. What can I do, I says, if she speaks to me? Not answer, I says? Keep out of her way, he says. How can I, I have to clean her room, I says, and he clipped my ear for cheek, and so did Cook on the other side.

So I am writing this book while Hannah is ironing Cook's

aprons in exchange for me teaching her. She does not do the frills as neat as me, but Cook can just put up with it.

Friday, 26th July

Building Committee has accepted Master's design! We got another bottle of port.

Colonel Sibthorpe, the old MP, is raging in The Times. England will be overrun by the scum of the earth, thieves and vagabonds, ruined by the importation of cheap foreign goods, anarchy, epidemics of hideous foreign diseases, and lots more. Billy done a topping mimic of him, spluttering and roaring against gaslights and the electric telegraph and everything new. Cook laughed till she split a seam.

Saturday, 27th July

When I was brushing the carpet I noticed 3 brass stair rods gone. If Mrs McK or Major had come down first they could have slipped and broke their neck. They was there when we come down earlier. Found them (the rods) hid in a cupboard. Must have been Mr E, little d***l.

Sunday, 28th July

Learned about said, not says, and lie and lied and lay and laid. Miss L is ever so clever, far better nor our old teacher at school.

Monday, 29th July

Master has hired a hansom cab to come every morning at ½ past 5 for all day, as he needs a carriage right at hand and stabling in Town is very dear. Tom Tomlinson, the driver, is handsome and keeps his cab clean, a fine 2-wheel rattler, smart and fast, and his horse is a high-stepping bob-tailed hack, very shiny and bells on the bridle. But Cook saw me looking at him and pulled me in by the ear. You're too young yet for that lark, she said.

Mary was looking too, but Cook just tutted. She is 5

years older nor me, Mary, I mean. She has 3 followers as calls at the kitchen door for her, she goes out with them in turn and none of them knows about the rest, she says, but I wonder! There is Achitophel Jacoby, 2nd footman in Sir Robert Bligh's, but they calls him Jacob. Who ever heard of a footman called Achitophel? And Walter Cartwright, the fishmonger's son, and Harry Owens as is a Corporal in the Welsh Fusiliers, I think. But she is not serious about none of them. Cook said if she isn't careful she will get into trouble. Walter smells fishy, and Mary makes fun, singing, *Walter, Walter, lead me to the altar – but not by the hand!* Achitophel is tall and handsome, and has a nice laugh. But I like the Corporal, his red uniform and shiny buttons is lovely, and his beard is all curly and soft. Wonder if it tickles.

Dad would say God will punish me for sinful thoughts.

Tuesday, 30th July

Master is in Town again, never away just now! Cutting the ground for the new hall started even though they have still not got proper permission, putting in base plates for the columns. Has to be done exact, but Master said Mr Fox is a master engineer, knows precise what he wants and his draughtsmen can draw out Master's designs perfect for the ironfounders to cast the huge beams.

Everybody has been laughing about it for a year, the Exhibition I mean, with jokes in Punch and the music halls about Prince Albert begging round doors to get the money for it. (The Queen give a lot of her own money.) But now it is going ahead, they all look silly.

Friday, 2nd August

Mr B's turn. Mr E got into Mr B's pantry after luncheon. He hadn't locked it, Mr B, I mean, as is his duty, to keep the bottles safe from us thieving servants! So he took out a bottle of Madeira, Mr E did, as had been opened to refill the decanters, went behind the settee in the parlour, and finished the bottle. And Major and Mrs McK come down after their naps at 4 o'clock, and 3 ladies called for tea, and said, ever so delicate, Have you noticed an unusual odour, dear Mrs McKenzie? And a noise? So they looked and found Mr E snoring flat out, drunk as an Irish navvy, and sick all over the carpet, as I had to scrub, and Mrs McK all embarrassed in front of her friends. Lucky it wasn't brandy, I suppose, that would have killed him.

So Mary and me carried him upstairs and made him sick again with mustard and water and a feather. Served him right. So he will be whipped tomorrow when he is recovered enough to feel it. Good. But the Major is not strong enough yet to salt his tail proper. Should ask Mr B, he'd lay it on, he is in trouble too.

Saturday, 3rd August

Mr E feeling very sorry for himself and quiet. Good.

Tuesday, 6th August

Miss L interested in my family now she has met some of them. Told her about Jake as is 2 years older nor me, and Betsy and Ben 2 years below me, and then the babies as died with whooping cough and just wasting away, and then Davy as is just 5. And about my granddad encouraging the Master to put forward his ideas for building the 1st glass Stove House at Chatsworth, when he was Head Gardener and Granddad under him, so the Duke of Devonshire could grow oranges and pineapples and such like, and then when the glass fell off the cart Jake was lamed in his ankle and Granddad cut and got lockjaw and died. Miss L shivered, and said, Like the bear children, but real! Ooh, how horrible! I am so sorry! She was not really, but she was being polite.

So I told her how when Mr Paxton become superintendent of all His Grace's estates, and His Grace's friend, and rich and a Member of Parliament and on the Railway Boards and everything, he paid for me and Jake to go to school for 5 years. Teacher was fierce, welted our bums proper with his birch rod, for fidgeting or not learning our Bible verses or just him having a sore head! Miss L giggled like anything, don't know why.

Then I told her as how Master took me on as housemaid, but when Dad was sacked Master was off on business for His Grace and Madam away too, and Dad thrown out of the tied cottage and had to move to Town. And Master felt bad about it, when he come back, so he paid £20 to get Jake apprenticed to a cabinet maker, Smee & Son, a proper firm as will teach him good work, not an attic-master as bangs up rough chairs and such all cheap. And Jake was always angry because of being lame, but is happy now, learning to cut veneers and do fine marquetry as he can sit at, and his hands hardened now for the sawing. But he is still angry underneath, and swears as he will pay it back when he is a journeyman, he will not be beholden.

Mr B come looking for me, and rowed me again for gossiping. It is not my place to talk to the Family. Blah blah. Skinny sniveller.

Hope he never reads this!

Wednesday, 14th August

Billy has got a new pup, and called it Chopper. It's better nor Ratter, killed 3 mice and 4 roaches in the kitchen first night – and not so snappy. And more tail! Miss L likes it, and takes it for walks. Mr E started to tease it, but she said to him, Leave it alone, Edgar, this one might take off your nose! And he sulked off.

Tuesday, 20th August

Day off. Miss L did not come today, thank God. Cook give me half a bag-pudding to take home. She is not stingy with leftovers, lots would rather throw them out. Does not cheat neither, uses the 2 pints of cream she is allowed and gets good meat, not cheap and then split the difference with the butcher and hash it up so Mrs McK will not know. Cook is a good example, and I like her, though she clouts my ear when I peeve her.

Jake is not well, real nasty cough. Mam says it's all that fine sawdust in his throat. But I know she is scared it is the lung rot like Dad.

Her neighbours is all right, most of them, just skint. But there is one slut across the landing, Slack Annie, and her man and their gang, rowdy bullies. What can you do, when you are poor you got no choice.

Thursday, 19th September

Madam's young sister Miss Virginia – Mrs Rolland now I mean – and her husband come to stay with 8 trunks of clothes, to get some new dresses made, she says. Mr Rolland is richer nor Master. Mrs Rolland's snooty dresser Angelique come too, all Frenchy and says we've to call her Mamzelle Duval. Cook said, Mamzelle Duval? Dresser? Over my dead body! She's a plain lady's maid, her name's Annie Duncan, I know her mam in Brixton! Mamzelle Duval? Angelique, we'll go that far, but that's all! I can't be doing with putting on airs, Cook said. But we will not tell Mrs Rolland, who is snobby.

She is sharing our room, Angelique I mean. It is very tight with 4 of us but Cook will not share with a maid, special not a fake French one. She is snobby too.

Mrs R will give her old dresses to Angelique to sell. I had my eye on a dark green merino wool, but Cook wants it though she will have to let it out a mile.

Mr E is quiet, but I don't trust him.

Thursday, 26th September

First column being put up today for the Exhibition Hall, so the Family took a cab, a big 4-wheel growler, to see it. Miss L says as it is beside Rotten Row where the nobs ride, looking over the Serpentine.

First time Mrs McK has been outside in 2 months. She is very nervous, and not well, and of course ladies in an interesting condition, as the gentry says, don't like to be seen out. Major is better but still not well neither, up 1 day and down 10, and the bedroom like an oven – Billy says as he has 3 elbows in each arm with carrying up the coals.

Colonel Sibthorpe still ranting in The Times. Feel sorry for his wife. Billy would make a cat laugh, playing him.

Saturday, 5th October

Tutor hired to come in the mornings for Mr E and Miss L. Mrs McK says as Mr E is sickly and can't go to school till next year. I think he is fine, but she thinks he will be bullied. Hope so. The tutor is Septimus Pledge, tall and thin and studying to take Holy Orders as the Anglicans say, but had to leave to look after his mother as is ill. Mary tried to charm him but he never noticed, she was peeved.

Tuesday, 8th October

Coals spilled all down the stairs, dreadful mess. Billy got rowed, but he says it wasn't him. Mr E, for sure. Nobody saw him, but we know.

Wednesday, 9th October

Mr E bumped Hannah in the kitchen. She put her hand on the hot stove and burned it, but not too bad. Cook glared, and he says, Sorry, sorry, sorry! But he was grinning, and I knew he didn't mean it.

Sunday, 13th October

Learned about than, not nor.

Monday, 14th October

My day off tomorrow. Miss L come in while I was cleaning her room, and said as she wants to come again. I argued, hard as I could, but she insisted. I said, What would your mama say, Miss? Miss L said, She'll never know, she sleeps most afternoons while I take Chopper for a walk in the park, and Edgar doesn't come of course, lazy little pig. And if you don't take me, I'll go anyway, and probably get lost, and that would be worse! So I said, All right, Miss, but you meet me round the corner, and no earrings this time! And she said as we can take a cab there as well as back, so as not to lose time. Nice to have money.

Her mama would have a fit, but she will do it. I knew as she was going to be trouble, but it does cheer Mam up. Last time she said as I was right not to bring her – Miss L I mean – but she felt flat, she had tidied special and got in some tea.

Tuesday, 15th October

Nobody noticed Miss L, I don't think. She don't seem to care about the stink nor the dirt. She said she's seen worse in India, and disease too. Betsy has red-eye. Told Miss L not to touch anything, for if she got it, that would just put the kybosh on things. She gave Mam 2/- to buy mercury ointment for Betsy. She was very polite and Mam couldn't bring herself to refuse, even if it was charity.

Mam said as Jake's cough is no better, but he is bright

and enjoying his work. Mr Smee come into the workshop the other day with drawings for furniture as he is putting into the Exhibition, and told Dodds the foreman the veneers must be cut perfect, but Dodds said, Hicks has a steady hand and does fine work, so Mr Smee said, Well, I'll trust your judgement. Pleased Jake no end.

Miss L tried jellied eels. Was sick, but at least not on her clothes. Maybe she'll not come again.

Wednesday, 16th October

Family is going to go every week to see the Hall being built. Crowds of people are going, it is a great sight, they are lifting 200 columns a week, and putting in glass already, with more than 400 glaziers, and huge sheets – 4 foot by 2 foot, Miss L thinks. 400 tons of glass they will need, that's 300,000 panes – can't imagine that number.

Mary wondered how the big sheets was made, and I read her an article in the Illustrated London News. They melt sand and stuff in a furnace to make the glass, and work in teams – 2 ordinary glassblowers and 1 master and 4 or 5 boys. The boys gather a big blob of glass on an iron tube and take it to a blower as blows it up like a bladder. Then they take it

41

back and heat it up again, and bring it to the master blower, and he stands over a long pit and blows more, very even, and swings the glass at the same time, so it stretches into a long, fat sausage with straight sides. Then the boys take it and heat it again, very careful not to crack it, and cut off the ends and slice it down one side, and open it out flat. A good team can make dozens in a day and earn good money.

Saturday, 19th October

Miss L never caught the red-eye, thank God. But Mr E has it. Don't know how. Doctor said bathe it with hot salt water, and he screamed till his mama near fainted. Miss L has not let on that it could have come from Mam's house, God bless her.

Mr B said Mr E is being good now and I don't need to keep this record, but I like writing it. Mr B thinks it will make me and Hannah get uppish and forget our place, but Cook said as she likes to see young people try to get on in the world. Like the Master, she said, as stuck Mr B for an answer. Her and Mr B is glinting at each other about it. Cook is a bit of a Radical, I think.

Hope she never reads this or she'll clip my ear again.

Sunday, 20th October

Mr E didn't come to church today what with the red-eye and all, and while we was all out he called Billy to put more coal on the school-room fire, and then poked it himself, and some fell out on to the rug. So he yelled, and Billy come running back up and scooped up the burning rug with his own hands and the shovel and shoved it into the hearth.

So when we got back, Cook was wrapping his hands in butter paper, and Mr E was crying and blaming Billy. But Cook knew as how Billy had been downstairs before Mr E started shouting. So Mr E is in trouble again, for near burning down the house, and is never to be left in again on his own.

Billy was given a sovereign reward. Worth a few burns, he said, Mr E can set fire to the house any time for me!

And Mr B is shut up about Mr E being good now.

Monday, 21st October

Billy went out on an errand and has not come back. With his sovereign. Cook thinks as he has been robbed and killed.

Tuesday, 22nd October

Hannah found Billy blind drunk on the doorstep this morning and called me. I put him on his straw pallet in the cellar and told her to keep quiet, maybe he would recover without anybody noticing. But he come reeling out into the kitchen this afternoon, silly clod. Mr B was going to beat him, but Cook said as he would not feel it. So he was put back to bed, but would not like to be him tomorrow!

Wednesday, 23rd October

Billy thrashed, but not dismissed. Mr B said a sovereign was too much to give a lad, 5/- would have been plenty, and it was partly the Major's fault for tempting him. Mr E's too, Cook said, so we won't say nothing to the Family.

Family at Exhibition Hall again. Queen and Prince Albert come most weeks to see it too, and the Duke of Wellington every second day, near as often as Master.

Miss L said the floorboards are made already – big squares of slats to let the dirt get brushed through between – and being used now to protect the glass at the bottom of the walls while the men are working round. Trust the Master, it is all planned out.

Mr E fooling about again and scared a carthorse. Got trodden on, and sworn at by the driver, and Major was astonished that the man was fined by his foreman, and nobody argued. But he is angry all over again with Mr E. Good.

Tuesday, 29th October

Mrs R wanted some tape, but Billy was out and Mary has the red-eye now so Miss L offered to go if I come with her – her mama will not let her go out alone except to the park, she says it is not safe with all the workmen. So we went out, and she (Miss L) said, Come on, Lily, never mind the nearest shops, I'll say we misunderstood if anybody asks, we'll go to Harrod's and you can see what's happening.

So we nipped across from Harrod's new shop as they are building special for the Exhibition, to see the Exhibition Hall. Enormous. I never realized. It's as long as Charles Street, and as wide as the road and all the houses on both sides! All them columns like a forest, but delicate, tied together like a spider's web with smaller bars. Heavy horses everywhere, bringing in carts with the girders and timber, and helping haul them up into place, not scared by the din, sawing and clanging and shouting and 4 steam engines as works the cutting and drilling machines. 1,000 glaziers and 100s of others, with tents for them and their wives and horses, and piles of wood and iron and glass. Piemen are making a fortune!

Spoke to some of the men – Miss L is shy about speaking to strange men, but they was all polite enough. They can earn as much as 6d an hour, so in a week they make 28/- or 30/- – 10 times as much as me! But with all the crowds of men and all this money, there is no drunkenness nor no fighting. Colonel S must be disappointed. Everyone is working like the blazes to finish in time, and Mr Fox, the contractor from Birmingham, is there 14 hours a day.

Sunday, 10th November

Saw Mr E go into the parlour, and he was emptying the ashtray over the carpet. Just stood and looked at him, and he went red and giggled, and ran out. Brushed it up before anybody saw. Little swine.

Learned about come and came, and run and ran. Past tense they are called.

Tuesday, 12th November

Day off. Miss L came home with me again, told her mama she was out for a walk – wicked but what can I do? Mam likes her, and when it comes over her she seems that grown-up you cannot argue with her, no more than with Madam. Well, I can't anyway.

Girl called Birdy Stiles runs a mob of young thieves, real villains, as is always bullying Ben. They took a tray of pies off him last week as he was beaten for losing. One of them saw us leaving, but I hope he thought as Miss L was another servant. She had a plain jacket on, and a shawl over her head.

Mam said as Jake is better. Him and his mate Freddy is working on a pile of orders come in for cases and stands for the Exhibition. Mr Smee's furniture is the fanciest ever, Jake says, a bed of carved mahogany and a cabinet with pictures of vases of flowers made of rosewood and ebony and boxwood and 100 more kinds of wood as I can't remember the names of, all different colours like as if they was painted – wonderful Mam says – and curved glass doors at the ends.

Wednesday, 13th November

The Hall glaziers have a little carriage, big enough for 2 men and 2 boys. Runs in tracks along the gutters to let them put up the glass easy and fast. Miss L said Mr E climbed into one to get a ride, and the men were angry because they were trying to beat the record of 420 sheets in a day, and he interrupted them. They threw him out, and he stamped his foot and swore, and Major was annoyed and said he needs licking into shape. More power to his arm, we say.

Mr B said as Punch magazine is calling the hall the Crystal Palace. The Committee don't like it, but we all think it's a fine name.

Saturday, 16th November

Mr E came into the kitchen for some cake. Cook has given him plenty before, and so he has played no tricks on her, but today she told him, Your mama says as you're to get no more because of not eating your dinner. He took a spat and yelled heathen words, and broke 3 bowls quite deliberate. One was chipped already but one was the good blue china one full of cream, and Cook had to make an eggy custard for dinner instead. When Mrs McK asked, Why is there no cream? Mr B said all polite, An accident in the kitchen, Madam, and slid his eyes to Mr E. Her face went all tight, he said, and she just said, Very well, Bibbings.

So Mary says as we can blame accidents on Mr E. Serve him right.

Tuesday, 26th November

Mr E spilled ink over Master's desk, and Major told Mr B to get new blotting paper before Master knew. Billy was out on an errand already, so Mr B sent me. Went to Harrod's shop of course, and nipped over to see the Crystal Palace again. Marvellous! Master calls the glass sheeting a tablecloth, but it's more like a layer of diamonds, up & down zigzag like a concertina. So many people going to visit, they are charging 2/- to get in to see it. The money is paid to men hurt in the building or to their widows.

Mr B rowed me for taking so long. Worth it, though.

Wednesday, 27th November

Master went with the Family to the Crystal Palace today, and when the crowds recognized him they cheered him, like they do the old Duke of Wellington. He says the crowds are slowing the workmen. Don't know how they could go faster; Pickfords vans is delivering tons of columns daily, and 300 columns is erected every week, and their girders fastened safe even in pouring rain. But the Master always expects more. They work till midnight every night, with bonfires of wood shavings for light.

Friday, 29th November

Madam has come for a week, to get things for Christmas. Lot of work making sure her room is clean. She is a stickler, but fair, said she has good reports of me. Made me feel good.

Monday, 2nd December

This morning Mrs McK caught her heel on a torn flounce in her petticoat and fell downstairs. Mary and me carried her back to her room, and Madam sent Billy running for Dr Bryce. She is all bruised and shook up, and has a sprained ankle and arm, but there's no bones broke. But she is to stay in bed for a few days. Angelique has offered to repair all her clothes – truly Christian as it is not her job. She is nicer than Cook thinks. Pretty name, Angelique.

Later

Great news! Mrs McK's baby is born, a month early after her fall. Madam sent Billy racing for the doctor again, but Baby came all in a rush. Well, it was her 9th. Lucky her and me both knew what to do. Madam had dinner guests to see to, and Angelique was useless, flapping like a wet hen, and Mary was needed to serve at table – but it all went quick and easy.

Nothing ready, no cot nor nothing. Had her clean and wrapped up (my shawl!) before the doctor arrived.

Baby has dark downy hair and bright blue eyes, just 4lb 6oz – perfect but very small. Dr B said Mrs McK must stay in bed for a month, not just 10 days like is usual for ladies. She is tired out and weak, and the doctor is sending in a wet nurse, because she can't feed the baby herself (though she wanted to as is not the fashion with ladies) and cow's or goat's milk is not safe.

Mary says when I slapped Baby to make her cry they heard her downstairs. Hannah had a laughing fit with excitement and Billy slapped her! And in the fuss Chopper jumped on the table and licked all the cream swirls off the dessert, but Cook piped on some more and the guests never noticed. She told Billy, If that dog ever comes in my kitchen again except at night he'll go out of it in a pie!

Cook and Mr B drank a glass of the sweet Madeira wine she puts in the trifle, same as usual, and gave me one too. You need it, Lily! Mr B said, with the biggest grin ever. Nicer than port.

But better than that, Madam called me when the guests was all gone, and said she was pleased with me because they never noticed the fuss, and the baby is safe. Gave me a gold sovereign! And then Madam said the doctor says I did well, considering. Considering what? I said, that Madeira making me bold. I helped Mam with our Davy and the other babies,

I said, before I was 10. So Madam asked me about helping Mam, and looking after Betsy and Ben and Davy, and she said she had arranged for a nanny to come from the agency next week, but she don't think she'd do any better, so I'm the new nanny! At £6 a year, like Mary, and a uniform, of course. And there will be a new housemaid hired.

But I must not drink no more Madeira.

Angelique will have to move in with Cook, to let the new girl in with Mary and Hannah and me. Cook will be mad. She says Mrs McK is saving £4 a year by having just me, instead of a proper nanny. But I don't care, it is still £2 a year more while the McK's are in England, as might be long enough with Major still not too good.

Tuesday, 3rd December

Mrs Coppy the wet nurse is a costermonger. She says wet-nursing is a rest from working on her market barrow, and her man can run it in the meantime. Do him good, she says, the lazy d***l! Her own baby died 2 days ago, but she don't seem to care much, it was her 14th and only 2 had died before. She said she felt like the Old Woman as lived in a Shoe. Babies poppin' out me ears like rabbits, she said, made us all laugh. Her oldest girl (as is 10) is looking after the rest.

Cot and everything is delivered, and I got the nursery set up. Room is big, and I am to sleep there with Baby and Mrs C, so the new maid can have my bed and keep Cook happy. She is Cockney (Mrs C) and Billy has to translate what she says, we can't hardly understand her. Which is maybe not a bad thing as she is very coarse and swears a lot, and Cook said we mustn't listen to what she says about followers, and such. She is not married to Mr Coppy. She says costers don't hold with it, why should a man own what his wife earns with her own work and brains and barrow? I never heard of such a thing, God will punish them.

Wednesday, 4th December

Baby is fretful, but it is just because she came early. Madam and me think she will get better as she grows. Have to keep her very cosy and soft and dry, and not disturb her more than I can't help nor let Miss L and Mr E neither. Madam is staying on till Mrs McK is better.

Thursday, 5th December

Madam took Miss L and Mr E to see the Crystal Palace. (Major is not well, he is always up and down with his wound.) Starting to put up the big half-circle ribs for the arched transept. Miss L says they are huge, and must be lifted by men, being as horses are not trusted to be steady. 11 men haul at pulleys on each corner. The ribs are a bit wider than the passage, so they has to be tilted and then lifted, each corner a few inches in turn, and then when they're right up, turned level and lowered on to rollers on top of the walls, and slid into place. Any slip could smash columns and glass all along a side. What a cheer, she said, when each is bolted down safe! Even Mr E was impressed.

Friday, 6th December

New maid, Jinny Nunn. Big and clumsy and dozy and sly with it. Mr B has scolded her already for laziness. Got Nunn sense, if you ask me.

Tuesday, 10th December

Madam had said for me to have my day off today, because it is due the day before Christmas when we will all be so busy, but said this morning as I had to miss it, as Baby is so new and frail and Mrs McK still wobbly, and Mrs C a stranger, and liking her gin, though Madam don't know that. Madam gave me 2/-, and will let me have another day later. Sent Billy with a note to Mam, very considerate. Away all afternoon – said he got lost, but Mr B said he was skiving and clouted him.

Thursday, 12th December

Baby christened this morning, Victoria Grace, in compliment to the Queen, and the Duke has graciously agreed to be her godfather. I was hoping for a big do, but Mrs McK is still weak and Baby should not go outside yet, so Reverend Pinkney came to the house. Madam lent her own lace christening robe, lovely. Baby cried all the time, annoying but lucky.

Looking after Baby and cleaning just the nursery is easier than being a housemaid. Lots of little clothes to wash and iron, but not such heavy work. Tiring, though, waking at all hours of the night to Baby.

Sunday, 15th December

Madam said we have to keep the house very quiet, and specially Baby at night, so the Major can sleep, he is still unwell. Which is hard being as Baby cries so often, and Mrs C swears like a trooper if she is wakened. Very tired.

Wednesday, 18th December

Gripe water don't stop Baby crying. Mrs Coppy gets Billy to bring her gin, a bottle a day. She said, Give the babby a drop on your lean (that is lean and linger, as means finger) and she'll sleep. So I did, and she only woke once for feeding, right through till breakfast. Wonderful!

Mrs R has 6 lovely new dresses, 1 maroon grosgrain, all

ruches, and another fawn sateen with fringes and pink ribbon roses, and coats and bonnets. Angelique sold me a deep pink chip straw hat with ribbon and lovely cock feathers for 2/- (3 guineas new). It goes lovely with my green Sunday skirt and black jacket. And a brown check linen dress and tan coatee with matching braid, ever so stylish – 8/-, and only 2 or 3 hours' work to make it fit perfect. That's 3 sets of clothes I have in my chest, as well as my uniforms for work!

Mrs McK is getting stronger. Took Baby in to her for a few minutes in the afternoon. She is better while she is in bed, not so nervous. Safe from Mr E, I think.

Mr E keeps creeping up behind Jinny and tugging her apron strings undone, and especial when she has her hands full. She cries. She is a dismal lump. He has not tried anything too bad recently – that is just plain naughtiness like any boy. Don't blame him really, could do the same sometimes just to wake that dough-head up.

Friday, 20th December

Have to use the gin most nights, Baby is so fretful. Mrs C just laughs and says, Never done none of mine no harm. Not happy about it, though.

Tying holly and ivy and rosemary on all the pictures and banisters ready for Christmas. Even Jinny is smiling and working. Master and Madam have gone home for Christmas with their children. They're coming back for a big party on Boxing Day, and Lord Granville and His Grace may come. Madam bought one of them German trees as Prince Albert has made all the rage, and Mr E and Miss L spent 15/- in Harrod's buying candy canes and coloured glass balls and red and gold ribbon. They did not do this in India.

Fruit for the mince pies is steeping in spices and brandy. Whole house smells lovely. Cook is doing a simple Royal Roast for the party. Queen Victoria (or her cook more like!) stuffs boned birds inside each other – a lark in a blackcock in a quail in a partridge in a pheasant in a duck in a capon in a goose in a turkey (could have missed some!). We are having only 5 kinds, up to a goose.

Mrs McK got up today for a while after luncheon, and sat in a wrap by the window to look at the street. Said she could not come down, not with so many important people coming to see Master, all sorts from all over the world, with problems and questions and things as they want to display in the Hall.

Mr E dropped a box of glass balls as shattered all over the parlour carpet, took Jinny ages to brush up all the splinters. But we think it was probably an accident, and give him the benefit of the doubt.

Later

Have to write this though it is nearly 2 in the morning, I am that angry! Baby wouldn't settle, and cried and cried – even gin did not help. Then I remembered Mr E had come in the nursery after Baby's bath, while I was ironing, to kiss Baby goodnight before he went to bed, or so he said. And he was grinning. So I looks careful in Baby's clothes, and tucked down her back inside her vest is a prickly holly leaf. No wonder the lamb cried! Her little back is all red marks like with fleas. I shall strangle that boy one of these days.

Monday, 23rd December

Mr E stayed well clear all yesterday, but this morning he came in with Miss L, thinking she would protect him. But I sent Mrs C down to the kitchen for a cup of tea and spoke to him, polite but firm. That holly was a nasty, cruel trick, Mr Edgar, I said, and if I have any more trouble from you I shall tell your mama and Madam both, spit spot I shall! My knees were shaking, rowing the young master, but I did it.

He was not ashamed of himself nor sorry, he just blushed because I said it in front of Miss L, and then he was angry enough to spit, and started shouting Indian words, but Miss L was shocked and slapped him and said, Don't you call Lily that! I'll tell Mama myself! And she rowed him too for hurting Baby, far worse than I did. So he went quiet, and I asked her not to tell, so long as there was no more trouble. But she made him apologize to me.

He looks as if it was him would strangle me if he could.

Nice bright crisp day, so took Baby out for a walk in the park for the first time, just for a few minutes and well wrapped and cosy. Helped me recover. Some of the other nannies spoke to me, ever so kind, said Baby is pretty, and if I need advice just ask. I started to sit on a bench in a good sunny corner, but they warned me that's where Nanny Devonshire and Nanny Marlborough and them sit and any untitled baby's nanny as dares sit there gets chased sharpish. On my way back, saw one little boy hitting another, and when the second one's nanny went to stop it, the bully's nanny was horrified. How dare you touch him, he's the son of a duke! she said.

Bought one of the new greetings cards for Miss L from a barrow on the way back, a rose wreath. Mam has made her a Christmas gift of silk gloves with a flower embroidered

on the cuff – she only had to pay for the pieces from her
work boss.

Wednesday, 25th December

New uniforms for Christmas as usual, and 6 pair of black
stockings, and cotton to make aprons. Mary and Jinny and
Hannah and me got Saxe blue, and Mary a neat black for
afternoons as well, and lace to trim her afternoon aprons.
Cook got black too. I got a navy wool coat and bonnet with a
Saxe-blue ribbon for walking out with Baby, and also 3 yards
of spotted light-blue calico as will make a lovely blouse and
frills. Mary said, It matches your eyes, you'll look pretty. Not
as pretty as you, black suits you, I said, as pleased her.

Miss L give me a pen wiper she made herself with a lily
painted on it. For your writing, she said. She likes the gloves.
Mr E sulked because I hadn't got him nothing, but he don't
deserve it.

Baby has slept right through these last 2 nights with no
gin. Good. She is growing fast.

Family just had a quiet Christmas dinner and early bed to
rest for tomorrow's party. But we had a slap-up dinner in the
servants' hall – a goose, with wine, and port after, and brandy

burning over the pudding. I carried Baby downstairs instead of eating in the nursery as usual. Mr B made a fine speech about the Crystal Palace and how him and me are proud to work for as great a man as Mr Paxton, and I said, Hear, hear! Then he said we have to toast the Major too, for he is a hero as was wounded fighting for Queen and Country. And health to him and Mrs McK, and all their children. (He stressed *all* and we all giggled when Billy booed but Mr B frowned him quiet.) And then to the Queen and Prince Albert, and then others as I can't remember, and Cook's face turned crimson, and Jinny slid under the table. I just couldn't stop giggling, but Hannah was sick.

So I come away. As I went up the stair I saw the green door was a bit open, and Mr E behind it in the hall in his nightshirt, spying on our fun. He run off back up the stairs and into his papa's bedroom. So I nipped back to warn Mr B, and when Major rung for him a minute later he had his coat and tie on and his face washed and hair combed, all tidy, and could go up right off, sober as could be expected at Christmas. So the little imp was foiled again, trying to get us into trouble on Christ's birthday. He is just full of malice.

Thursday, 26th December

My head is a bit heavy. Hannah says she is fine, but Cook with a hangover is snappier than old Ratter, and always slapping Jinny for being useless. Nothing new in that, I said.

Master and Madam came up by train this morning, for the party tonight. I helped Miss L dress, in tartan taffeta with bright green sash and braid. Mrs McK said she is old enough to go down for 2 hours, and she would just stay a short time herself. Her own dress was grey silk with lilac swags, because she is still in half mourning for her babies in India. Madam has a new russet cut velvet with gold lace. Master looks very fine, in deep blue velvet with a roll collar, and Major a real swell in his uniform – Scotch kilt and tartans as Her Majesty likes, and silver buckles as Billy polished up like mirrors.

Mrs R wore sea-blue satin with silver flounces and bugle beads like foamy waves, and a new-fangled petticoat called a crinoline with a whalebone cage so wide she had to lift one side to get down the stairway. Dear me, how poky, Judith, she said all superior, a man there would see my garters! Mrs McK looked peeved.

Mr E was let come down too, in a kilt and little soldier's

jacket as he is ever so proud of, made by the regimental tailor in India. Mrs McK sent him and Miss L up to bed at 10, but she enjoyed herself so much she stayed on till 1. All the guests' dresses was lovely, and Mrs C and me watched from the landing while Mr B and Angelique and Mary helped them with their wraps and coats. Hannah and Jinny got their ears clattered for peeking from the servants' door instead of helping Cook.

26 at dinner and not half a tight squeeze, and Mr B in a lather carving, and 2 waiters hired for the night. 8 couples was dancing, and Madam and Mrs McK played the pianoforte. Master had hired a fiddler too, a gypsy, him and Mary was flirting something terrible when he went down for his dinner as was half his pay. Cook gave him and the waiters a bag home for their families as it was Christmas, but she watched to see they didn't nab no cutlery.

About 11 they all wanted to see Baby. I was in my new uniform, and Baby all ready in her lace christening gown. Baby did not wake up and looked ever so sweet. Lucky!

Mrs McK said, Baby is only alive because Lily helped me (which is not true but I could not argue), and the Duke gave me a sovereign. And while they was all cooing over Baby, one of the men guests give me a kiss, and asks me when was my day off? My face was like a beetroot! I said I was too busy with Baby to have followers, and they all guffawed, and he give me another shilling. Soon be rich!

When I told Cook and Mr B they laughed like jackasses and said I done right. Mary was peeved. He must have been drunk, she said. But I think she is jealous that a gentleman kissed me and nobody kissed her, even under the mistletoe, except Billy and Mr B and the waiters and the gypsy. Enough for anybody, I think!

Sunday, 5th January

Madam left for Barbrook yesterday.

Took Baby to church with the Family for the first time and Mrs McK said, You'll sit with us, of course, Lily. So I sat in the Family pew instead of at the back with the other servants. I was sinful proud, but God punished me, seeing as Baby screamed when the organ started and I had to take her out, everybody looking and Mr E sniggering like mad.

In the afternoon the Family went out to the Crystal Palace again. Miss L came into the nursery and told me about it. Her mama had said, I don't see how Joseph (that is, Master) can get it done in time. Well, Miss, I said, Mam says children and fools should not see a house half built or a thing half made. She laughed and said, It's as well Mama isn't here! She is nice, which is just as well, seeing as how I was being so cheeky. Mr B is right. Need to watch out or I'll get myself in trouble *without* Mr E's help.

Mr E splashed in the mud and got filthy, Miss L said, and her mama scolded him for naughtiness. It wasn't just naughtiness, I think, it was to give Billy and Jinny and Mrs Stevens the washerwoman more work. Miss L never thinks of that, of course.

Monday, 6th January

An officer from India called today to see Master, with a black man, a Hindoo, as was his friend. Captain James, as was the officer's name, had brought some Indian brassware home with him and they wanted to put it into the Exhibition. And the Captain knew Major, so they asked to give their regards to him and Mrs McK, and they all had tea together. Mary was ever so excited.

I had to take Baby down. The Hindoo was not real black (I seen lots far blacker round Mam's way). Very polite and gentlemanlike, he was, and his hands small and delicate. He wore an embroidered waistcoat, and a diamond ring and a big gold fob at his watch chain, and he had orange cloth wrapped round his head like a pumpkin. It's called a turban, Miss L says. He gave Baby a solid gold bangle from his own wrist. Washed it careful and Mrs McK has put it away for her.

Wednesday, 15th January

Mrs Coppy came back late from her evening off disgraceful sozzled, a real bucketful. She collapsed on the nursery floor with her skirts all skew-whiff and her wig fallen off into the fender. Mr E saw Mary helping her up the stairs, and ran and told his mama.

She come up. Disgusting! she said, I'll have Bibbings clear her out at once. Lily, you'll have to use cow milk till the doctor can send a new nurse.

Pardon me for saying so, Madam, I said, ever so polite, but cow milk is dangerous to babies, even if the man milks the cow right outside your door into your own container so as you know it is clean. And Baby is not yet that strong.

You can't mean you want her to stay! she exclaimed, exasperated. Well, Madam, I said, she is clean and healthy and very satisfactory to Baby.

When she is sober, Mrs McK snapped.

I had to nod, but I said, If you was so gracious as to give

her another chance I should admonish her most severe, Madam, and I'm sure she would feel ever so obligated for your beneficence and be vastly rectified in future. And she near started to giggle, snorting through her nose same as Miss L does sometimes. Then she said, Very well, Lily, but just this once, and then she run out. Gentry is odd.

Mrs C is snoring on the floor, like Billy last year. She can just lie there.

Thursday, 16th January

Mrs C's head splitting, stiff and aching. Rowed her like Madam once rowed a clumsy sweep as broke a mantelpiece, she is very sorry and promising to never ever touch another drop of gin. Maybe 2 weeks till the fright wears off.

Tuesday, 21st January

Dreadful day. Can't sleep, and I'm writing to calm myself. Hands shaking that much I'm making blots all over.

My afternoon off, so took Baby out in the morning. After luncheon saw Baby fed and dry and happy and clean, and left her with her mama to look after for me, and Mrs C there if she was needed, and well warned. Changed into my old brown skirt and jacket and black straw hat and shawl, and left at 2 to go home as usual.

In the street, there was Miss L waiting for me. Not again, I said! But she laughed. I said, You'll get me dismissed, but she said, No, no. And I said, Well, Miss, if you insist then I can't go, and it's not right you losing me my only time to go and see Mam. 2 till 5 I has, every 4th Tuesday, it's not a lot. But she said again, No, I'll say I ordered you, Lily, you couldn't help it. We'll get a hackney again, you'll have plenty of time.

So what could I say?

Just then Tom Tomlinson drove by, heading for the cab rank. Master being away in Manchester he is free, and she waved him down. Haggs Alley? he said. Off Paradise Lane? You sure, Lil? No place for a young lady. Tell Miss Laura, I said, I tried to stop her. And she said, Don't worry, I've been before.

While we was talking, Mr E ran up, and he wanted to come too! Miss L was angry, but I said, He's just saying the same as yourself, Miss! And we could not argue him out of it, so at last Miss L said, Very well, but behave yourself!

Tom was not happy. When we got there, he looked round the empty holes where shutters and doors had been broken

71

up for fires, and where pigs was rootling round an old beggar sleeping under a pile of rubbish, and he said, This it, Lil, girl?

And I said, Well, yes, for me. This is where Mam lives now, but I think as the young master and miss should go home, I really do. Silly Lily, Miss L said, laughing, and skipped out, pert and sweet, and Mr E after her, but he held his nose. So I said, Tom, come back for us at 4, promise! And he swore, Swelp me, I'll be here, Lil! And then he got out of it, with 2 brats hanging on under his seat at the back, but he flicked his whip down and knocked them off yelling.

Birdy Stiles and her mob were there. They came swarming round, and Miss L was alarmed and said, They look rougher than Indian children. Will they throw stones? No, no, I said, but come along quick!

Mr E was complaining loud and nasty. What a pong, he says. Look, rubbish and filth and a dead dog! Yes, I said, and a pigsty in that cellar and the stable for donkeys next to the pie shop, and no sweepers round here nor no sewers neither, I said, I told you not to come.

Then he jeered, Are these horrid dirty children your brothers and sisters, Lily? They're stinking and disgusting, poo!

I near hit him, but Birdy and her mates was drawing closer, and a few sluts too, all staring at the fine clothes. Even if Miss L's was plain in her book, they was better than anything round our way. I knew we were in trouble, so I got

Miss L and Mr E in and up the stair fast as I could. But I could hear feet pit-pat following us up the stair, quiet-like.

Mam said, Slack Annie's been passing comments about you, Miss, being rich. And she made a face. She's there, I said, and Mam went white and jammed the door with a chair, and said, Maybe they'll go away. But she didn't really expect that. None of the neighbours will help, she said, even the honest ones. There's just little Mr Dufresnay as writes pamphlets, and old Jim and Martha Wardle, and half-witted Jerry, and Pompilius Allen with the shakes and his mother, and one-legged Bakey down below. And them new-fangled Peelers, never one about when you need one!

Mr E was cursing in heathen at me and Miss L for bringing him. When the door rattled he screamed and browned his trousers which made him very ashamed. Outside Annie called, Let us in, let us in, Bessie Hicks, or it'll be the worse for you! And Mam just sat, and all of us. My heart was thumping fit to knock down the house. And Annie laughed, and snarled, You've got to come out sometime.

Miss L said, If I give them my purse will they let us go? How much is in it? I said. She tipped it out on the table. 3½ sovereigns and a dozen silver coins and some coppers. The children was all staring, they'd never seen so much money. But Mam said, No, Miss, they'll take it and then rip off your fancy clobber anyway. Miss L looked horrified. S'worth good silver in the flea market, I said, I *told* you you oughtn't have come.

73

You were right, Lily, she said, trying to smile, and I promise I'll listen to you in future. That's a first, I said joking, and she even chuckled. She has real courage, that one.

Mam said, I could give you old clothes. Oh, yes! Miss L said. Isn't this an adventure? All bright and brave, to keep Mr E's chin up – but her lips was white.

Mam found her an old skirt and blouse of mine as she had kept for Betsy, and a mob-cap and my shawl. Mr E got Jake's old trousers and shirt and waistcoat, and when he hesitated Mam said, They are clean, Sir, and he snarled at her and whimpered. But he put them on all the same, and a muffler too, and Ben's Sunday boots with paper stuffed in the toes. And we laid out the fancy things on the table.

By this time it was about 4, when Tom said he'd come back. So when the door rattled again, and strained in, Miss L and Mr E and me stood behind it, and Miss L and I took Mr E's hands, and I said, God help us all, please, amen, and gave Mam the nod, and she jerked it open. All them as was shoving against it fell in past us, shouting, and when they saw the clothes and started grabbing them we wriggled out under Mam's arm, keeping our heads low. When Birdy looked our way, I dropped the crown and pointed, and they started to fight for it, all bent down scrabbling. I did that 4 times, with silver and pennies, and that got us down the stair, all jostled but not hurt.

But the cab was not there.

So we started up the alley. I told Mr E not to cry and to walk steady, but he was scared. He tugged and began to scream. Then they chased us down the lane all screeching like after a thief, only it's usually them as is chased. Must have been 25 of them, children and women mostly. I tossed up the gold coins last, to glitter and tinkle, and they stopped, Annie and them, to fight for them, just what I hoped for, and jammed the alley. I yelled, We ain't got no more money, that's it all! But Birdy and her mob kept coming on. And the cab was still not there.

So we ran out on to Paradise Lane, past a brazier roasting chestnuts, and I kicked it over. Them behind burned their feet on the hot coals and started to yell and curse and dance, and some stopped for the nuts. And then Jake and his pal Freddy come walking towards us, and I yelled to him. They ran over, and we got into a corner so nobody couldn't come at us from behind, and when the mob came up, Jake and Freddy and me thumped them. Birdy punched me right in the eye and I kicked her, and Miss L was fighting too, screaming in heathen, and Mr E screamed too, behind us. Miss L was very brave. But there was too many of them and I thought we was done for.

And then a clatter and the horse came up galloping, and then rearing as Tom reined in till I thought as it was going over and its hooves flying and one boy got kicked in the face and he was thrown back, spitting teeth. Get in! Tom shouted, flogging the mob back. We heaved Mr E in, his legs flapping, and then Miss L and me, and Jake and Fred hung on the side, and Tom whipped up and away.

Mr E was quiet, for a mercy, and Miss L was laughing with fright past, and I was all shaking and sick. But at least we was safe.

Tom stopped after a bit, in a respectable street, and we sorted ourselves out. Jake started to cough, deep and hard, with a big splatter of blood. Freddy explained that was why they were out. Jake had collapsed, and Mr Davy had told Freddy to help him home, as was kind, most would have sent him off alone. Just the excitement kept him going during the fight. They went back from there, Freddy helping Jake.

When we got home, Tom tied his horse to a gas lamp and followed us in. The Major raged at me fiercer than I'd ever heard, and no wonder, what with me taking Miss L and Mr E to the slums and bringing them home in rags and half murdered, all dirty and crying, and all their money gone, and me with a black eye and bruised all over and my hair like a bush where somebody had pulled it.

But Miss L stood up for me like a hero. I made Lily take me, Papa, she said, I made her, so it's not fair to blame her, it's not her fault. We didn't know there would be any danger. And then Lily and her family, she said, they fought like lions to save us, they brought us home safe in the end.

She was crying, and no wonder. Even if she does act like a little lady most of the time she is young yet and I never saw nobody more red-faced with rage than Major McK, and panting with strain he was, he is not proper well yet. I was glad Miss L did not show her papa the bruises where she was kicked. And gladder still when she put a stop to Mr E's whining. She just said flat out, No, that is not true, Edgar. You made us take you just as I made Lily. And this brave man rescued us.

Tom said, Any man would've done, Sir, but it's right what Miss says, I 'eard the young gennelman say he'd scream if the girls left 'im behind, an' Lil tried hard to make 'em stay in the cab and let me take 'em home, honest she done. He is a good man, he might have been sent off for speaking out against Mr E.

So Major McK hesitated, and in the end Tom got a sovereign and went off happy. Miss L and Mr E were rowed something awful, and sent with Mary to clean up before their mama saw them. Major said, I don't want to worry your mama in her state of health. She has been sleeping quiet with Baby beside her all afternoon. We shall not mention this to her.

I got a tongue-lashing myself, of course, and a warning I'd be sacked if anything like it ever happened again. Can't complain, really.

But Mr B and Cook are angry that I risked the children,

77

and Mary because Tom stuck up for me, and Jinny is grinning like a Cheshire cat that it's me in trouble this time, not her.

And Jake is coughing blood. Says he'll be back at work in a day or so. Not if it's the lung rot he won't. And Mam in trouble because of me, though with £3 in their pockets Birdy, Slack Annie and her mates should leave her alone. But what could I have done?

Sunday, 26th January

Still shaking. Baby is well, and Mrs McK has never mentioned it. But she looks grim, so maybe Mr E has told her, trying to get me in trouble though his papa said to keep it quiet.

Freddy come to the servants' door this morning and said Slack Annie died raving drunk with gin Friday last. One worry less, I thought, and thanked him for fighting for us and helping Jake. Your mam's helped me since a cart run me dad over and the hospital killed him, he says, and I'll help you all I can, any time!

Snowed. Mr E and Miss L was thrilled, being as they never seen snow in India. After church they made a snowman in the street, very dirty with all the horse-droppings. They got rowed for it and for playing on a Sunday, but at least I wasn't involved this time. But somebody poured water on the servants' steps and it froze, and Jinny slipped and hurt her leg. We think it was Mr E.

Later

Such a commotion, Jinny is off! She was moaning about her leg, and Cook told me and Mary to help her up to her room and put her to bed. Mrs McK saw us and come up too, concerned, and said, It's cold up here, put a shawl round your shoulders. And she opened Jinny's box before Jinny knew, and lifted her shawl, and 3 silver teaspoons tinkled out as had been hidden inside it!

Sore leg? Mrs McK said. Sore back it'll be if you stay in this house one minute longer! Or would you prefer the police? Hanging it is, for over 40/- worth of goods, or 10 years' transportation to Australia!

And Jinny jumped up and dressed, crying like the village pump but her leg not sore no longer. Mrs McK told her to leave her uniform, as she didn't deserve it. She looked through her box and her pockets and found Miss L's tortoise comb and a silver card-case and a coral brooch of Angelique's and Mr E's Sunday cuff links. So Jinny was a thief, and stupid with it.

She must have known we'd have looked at her and Angelique as the last ones in as soon as things was missed. And she went off with her box, wailing. Don't know where and we don't care, dirty thief!

And Mr B said to me, At least you're honest, even if you haven't enough brain to keep your ears apart! Which is kinder than he has been for days, even though he is in trouble that she could have got the spoons out from under his nose as he is responsible for.

Mr E sneered, and said where we could hear him, You said you can't trust slaveys, Mama! But I still feel almost grateful to him and Jinny. At least it has taken people's minds off me.

Thursday, 30th January

Master is here to finish the Crystal Palace for handing over. Very busy, but he took time to speak to me about the fight at Mam's. I have to be careful in future. Which is as good as I could hope for. But he told Miss L and Mr E it is not right to get me into trouble, like I said.

Friday, 31st January

New housemaid, Peggy Boyle, Irish, just come to London on the train yesterday. Small and dark, don't know enough to keep out of the traffic, but a worker. Raised in a convent. Not her fault she is Catholic so we have to be tolerant, Mrs McK says. She is used to heathens of course.

Mr B just sniffed. He despises Catholics, and Irish even worse, and says the Irish navvies as digs the canals are dirty, slovenly, drunken heathen brutes. (Cook is glinting at him again, she has a nephew as is a navvy, but English of course.) He does not like Methodists like me much neither. (Mr B, I mean.) But Peggy was not in the door 10 minutes till she was dusting the banisters, saying they was a disgrace. Will she keep it up, and prove Mr B wrong?

Sunday, 2nd February

Mr E is looking at me all sullen. Maybe thinking how he disgraced himself at Mam's, and hating me for it.

Miss L is still helping me with my spelling and says she will help me speak better too, and write proper grammar. That isn't just using big words like I thought, it's how to put words together properly, to make people respect me as an intelligent and competent person. Sounds very posh, for a housemaid, but if I want to be Housekeeper at Chatsworth, I shall need to.

Cannot rewrite this diary, it has enough scribbles and scores as it is. So the wrong grammar will just have to stay. But I shall try to do better.

Monday, 3rd February

On the stair I heard Major tell Miss L as it is not fitting for a young lady to be too friendly with the lower classes. That means me. But Miss L said, Excuse me, Papa, but Mama is happy for me to help Lily. Aunt Sarah goes to read the Bible with poor people, every 2nd Thursday, as her charity. Teaching Lily is mine. How she stands up to her papa, polite but firm and ever so grown-up already. She will be a great lady some day! And her papa said, Very well, but only for her lessons! He does mind, but he is trying to be fair. Bit like Mr B with Cook. Must not get uppity or I'll get Miss L in more trouble.

Hard to balance between trying to improve yourself and get on in the world, and not forgetting your place.

Thursday, 6th February

Peggy talks and sings to herself all the time in a language called Gaelic. Thought that was them niffy French onion things. She is from a town called Cork, as made Billy laugh. She shouted at him, and he yelled, Go boil your cork, Boyle! as made her more angry, till Mr B shut them both up. Most of them in Cork (I think it's funny too) cannot speak much English. Queer to think of British people as can't speak proper. But then, there are all the people in India. But they are not British. Are they? Are the Irish British? (Mr B says yes about the Irish.)

Mr E has started imitating the Gaelic, not learning it, just making fun. It would make a cat laugh, but Peggy gets angry like with Billy. She had better watch out, servants has no right to get angry at the gentry, my dad found that out. Mr B is stiff with her, but anyone who works that hard and thorough will get into his good books soon.

Miss L says as Mr E is talking in his sleep, saying things like, I'll kill her! Only in heathen, that he was used to talk with his Indian nurse. She thinks he is talking about me. Scary, but he has done nothing.

Sunday, 9th February

Cook asked me now Baby is sleeping better to come down and read to them all again at night, while we are free to chat and do mending after dinner, like I did before Baby was born. When we first opened the house we started with Handley Cross, Cook's choice and very funny, about Mr Jorrocks, a stupid Cockney grocer as tries to become a gentleman. Mr B tried not to laugh because it made fun of the gentry too, but he couldn't help it. Then Mr B's turn, he chose a book of sermons, improving but boring. Mary picked The Horrible Mystery of Count Orlando the Vampire, as was gruesome but thrilling.

Hannah and Billy and me, we do not get a turn, nor Peggy nor Mrs C, and Angelique is not one of the Family. Think I should, being as I am Nanny now not just a housemaid, but Mr B says not yet. So Cook's turn again, and she has got The Vindication of the Rights of Women. Sounds all legal and dull as ditchwater, I must say. But maybe not. Didn't know as how women had rights.

Later

Such a row! Mr B nearly had a fit, shouted the book was immoral and revolutionary and unnatural, and the woman who wrote it was a disgrace to her sex, and she should be ashamed of herself corrupting us youngsters! (Cook I mean.) Cook was furious (I knew she was a Radical). Now they are passing messages to each other through Hannah, stiff as pokers the pair of them. We are all hiding our grins and being very polite.

Wednesday, 12th February

Yesterday Cook spoiled a caramel cream, and this morning the breakfast kidneys was scorched bad. Mr B just sneered. Mrs McK sent for her and rowed her and Hannah says her face is tight as a bag-pudding. Glad I'm away out of the worst of it up in the nursery.

Mr E slid downstairs on a tray and broke the tray and nearly his head, and got rowed, but just normal mischief.

Crystal Palace is handed over to the Commission. Colonel S said it wasn't safe, being as glass isn't thick enough and 10-to-1 it will shatter with hail or blow away in the wind. But it has stood firm under fierce storms this winter even before it was complete, so we all poo-poo him. And just to prove it was strong enough to hold the crowds they had soldiers in, marching and running and jumping all together and rolling trolleys loaded with tons of cannon balls about all the upstairs galleries. Master says as it is 3 times stronger than it need be, and he should know.

Friday, 14th February

Mrs McK is reading a book by Charles Dickens, called The Pickwick Papers, and she said she could not understand some of it, and showed it to me. I couldn't understand it neither, but when I tried reading it out loud, it was so funny we both started to laugh. The words is written just like they're said, so I could sound them out into sense, where Mrs McK could not because she don't know the way Londoners speak. Asked to borrow it to read downstairs when she has finished it.

Tuesday, 18th February

Afternoon off. Miss L did not come – what a relief! But Jake is very sick, coughing blood, and he can't scarcely stand. Shall pray for him. God's will be done, but it is terrible hard on Mam and the children.

Mr E has been very good for the last few days, has not teased Peggy nor Mrs C nor Hannah nor nobody, nor played no tricks, nor shouted at us. Working at his lessons too, Miss L says. Maybe he has decided being bad is more trouble than it is worth. Hope so, but I worry when he is good that he is planning something extra nasty.

Wednesday, 19th February

The Family is still going out to see the Palace, they can get in with Master being still involved. Miss L asked if she could bring Baby, so Baby could say later as she was there, and Mrs McK said no, carrying Baby was my job. Sly minx, Miss L, she winked at me, that was what she wanted! So I carried Baby very demure behind them and saw everything.

The pillars are so slim you don't scarcely notice them, I could near put my hands round them. They is set in 24-foot squares, being joined with cloth or wood walls to make 2 rows of big rooms each side of the wide middle passage, the nave like in a church. The 2nd storey is narrower, like a middle layer on a wedding cake, just one room each side, and balconies to walk along above the nave, that is open right up to the glass roof another step up. One staircase just at the cross is a double spiral, where people on it can see the whole length of both passages.

Different rooms for English goods, and for foreign things from all over, I don't know where half the places are. Col S says foreigners will steal all our manufacturing secrets, silly puffball. A secretary is busy listing all the 1,000s of exhibits, and soldiers on guard to see nothing is stolen. There's a huge American organ with an eagle on top and at one end tropical trees like a garden, and then blocks of stones, marble and slate – Raw Material exhibits. At the other end there's a place for Machinery and 5 steam engines to work them are hid in a big shed just outside to keep the noise down. 2 other sections – Manufactures and Sculpture/Arts – is mixed in all the rooms. Jake's employer's chair and sideboard are Manufactures, he says they should be Art. Bronze medals to be awarded to the best things in each section.

As we left the old Duke of Wellington himself arrived, a great supporter of the Palace like Prince Albert and Queen Victoria as visited just yesterday. Major said the Duke spoke to him last week about India where the Duke started soldiering 60 years ago. He was very proud to have spoken to England's Hero.

Monday, 24th February

Mr B and Cook can't be stiff when they are guffawing at The Pickwick Papers. Peggy does not understand much so we send her up to sit with Baby and let Mrs C come down, and she is in fits every night. It really shows how people talk, I shall try it.

Wednesday, 26th February

Nanny Pullings told me to wash Baby's head with boracic to cure cradle cap.

Crystal Palace again. Wonderful. Gas lighting, and a glass fountain like one of the crystal chandeliers from Chatsworth. I gasped when I saw it, How does it not break, it's so delicate! Major laughed, and said, Don't worry, Lily, it has iron rods hidden inside the glass tubes to hold it up, it won't fall on you! So maybe he has forgiven me.

The trees inside is all out in the warmth, and sparrows

nesting, droppings everywhere! Master was laughing about it, Mr B says. Someone had said, What if they s**t on the Queen? Panic! Somebody said the Guards could shoot the sparrows – but Her Majesty said wouldn't that break the glass? Sensible! Somebody else suggested bird lime, but it would make everything sticky. So Her Majesty wrote to ask the Duke of Wellington. He wrote back all stiff, I have the honour to be Commander-in-Chief of Your Majesty's army, not a birdcatcher! But he thought better of it, and told her, Try sparrowhawks, Ma'am!

Mr E very rude about a black man in the Africa room who was in a red hat and white tunic and trousers and gold sash and a big curved sword. He called him stupid Sambo just out of the trees, with a big pig-sticker to cut his toenails, thinking he would not understand, and then the man gave him a mouthful of oaths. Turned out he was a porter from Limehouse, and I near died trying not to laugh.

Thursday, 27th February

Boracic worked lovely, and Baby's cradle cap almost gone already. Has gained 4lb, and very pretty. Her baby down has all fallen, and dark hair like her mama's is growing in.

Saturday, 1st March

Mrs McK has asked me to go back to India with her. Don't know what to do.

Miss L says, Go, Lily, you must! There are so many young men, pick the right one and you could end up married to a colonel, or the governor of a district! Big house, servants. Better than I could do here. But also heat, flies, dirt, diseases, insects, snakes, loneliness, babies dying. Maybe Baby, how terrible! And I'd never be Housekeeper at Chatsworth.

Hannah did not come up, Mrs C's afternoon off. Baby sleeping. Glad of the peace to think.

Starched and ironed Baby's gowns. Frosty last night so I put them out on a bit of string across the window, can't do it during the day, Mr B would have a fit at clothes flapping in public! Nothing whitens small-clothes better than freezing them, not even rinsing in sour milk, and they are lovely now. No frost in India. Servants do all the work, Mrs McK says. Why does she need me? To see Baby don't grow up as spoiled as Mr E?

Wish she would go back to India and leave Baby here. Precious mite would have a better chance of surviving.

Madam and I would look after her like our own. Hard to leave all her children here, though. Can understand why—

Later

Mr E accused me of stealing. God burn him in eternal hellfire, amen.

That upset and angry I can scarcely write, these inky smudges is tears.

Mrs R went out shopping after luncheon. Mrs McK was reading and Miss L doing her 3 hours on the pianoforte. Mr E reading and restless, in and out as usual. Angelique went to polish Mrs R's silver ornaments, and run down to the parlour in a state. Brooch missing, she says, a big mourning one of gold and jet carved with lilies, with a lock of hair from Mrs R's baby as died.

Mr E said he heard me wishing it was mine when she wore it at an evening party. True, and Miss L had to nod. He said I could have decided to steal it and blame Jinny. Miss L said, No, Lily would not do that, but he said, How do you know? Slaveys are all liars and thieves, like Jinny. No they aren't, Miss L said, but he said, That's what Mama says, and Angelique says Mrs McK looked upset but it's true.

So she went up without calling me out of the nursery, I heard the bustle but never bothered, and searched my box as is kept in Cook's room now alongside Mrs C's, and the brooch was hid inside my new blue blouse.

So Mrs McK called me down to the parlour and accused me, in front of Miss L and Mr E, all sitting like judges in court, and Angelique too.

I near fainted. I said someone had put it there.

Angelique said as the brooch was kept in a small box inside the main jewel-boxes, just chance she saw it was not shut proper, it could have been missing for days. Trying to help.

Mr E said, But can she prove she didn't take it? The nursery is near Mrs R's room, and it would only take a second to slip along the corridor and lift it. And Miss L said, That is not enough. But he said, The brooch was in her box, and shrugged. And Mrs McK was wavering.

Then Mrs R came back, shocked when she heard. She said she nearly put it on to go out, so it was taken today. I said as I was in reading to Mrs McK before she left, and Mrs McK nodded. And then Mr B was coming out of Master's room when I was taking Baby back from her mama to the nursery, and saw me go right in there, and I remembered Mrs C was there and saw me started on the ironing before she went out.

But Mr E said, But you were alone with Mrs C out. Angelique, did you go downstairs at all? And Angelique had

94

to say, Yes, Sir, the servants always have a cup of tea at 3 just before tea goes up to the parlour. So, Mr E said in triumph, Aunt Virginia's bedroom was empty then and Lily could have got in easily.

But my jewel-boxes are kept locked, Mrs R said, frowning. Angelique, you did lock them when you left? And Angelique said, Yes, of course, Madam. But she blushed so we all saw she had forgot.

I protested as I had been ironing all afternoon, and writing my book. And that was the first I thought of it. So Mrs McK said she wanted to see it. Remembered all the things as I have been writing about her and the Family, and I did not want to show it, but she insisted. So she and Mrs R read through all the book, and looked at the ironing, and thought about it, while I could scarce breathe for fear and anger and shame.

Mrs R was peeved at some bits, and laughed – laughed! – at others, but Mrs McK was stiff, and upset, and embarrassed but trying to be fair. So at last she said, No, Lily, if you had just taken the brooch I do not believe you would have written as calmly as you did about going to India.

Especially considering all the other things she has written here, said Mrs R, I agree, she is not the guilty one. And they both looked straight at Mr E. And Miss L said, Edgar, you filthy horrid beast!

He was red as fire, and said, I just thought she might have.

And his mama said, No, Edgar, I think your Aunt Virginia

and Laura are right, it was someone who enjoys causing trouble, as is clear from this book.

Someone who knows about the servants' tea time, and knew he could go into my room then, and up to the attic, without being noticed, Mrs R puts in.

Someone who holds a grudge against Lily especially, Miss L sniped, all nasty.

Are we right? Mrs McK asked.

He looked shifty, and said, Maybe one of the other slaveys, Mama? And she said flat out, No, Edgar. Go to your room, I shall speak to your papa. And he slunk out.

And she said to me, That will be all, Lily. No apology nor nothing, but her hands was trembling.

So was mine.

I ran up to the nursery and cried all over Baby, and Mrs C was cursing in Cockney till Cook kindly sent Mary up with a glass of Madeira.

At last the Major came in, and nearly exploded, shouting, That damned brat! So he talked to Mr B and Mrs C and Angelique as had been rowed by Mrs R already for neglecting her duty, and pretending to be French as she had discovered in my diary. Then Major sent for me. Red and furious, but not with me. He said as he agreed with his wife, that I did not take the brooch, and gave me my book back and a sovereign. And sent us all downstairs and then whipped Mr E, we could hear him screaming even through the baize door. Serve the little rapparee right, Cook said, should have been done years ago, and weekly since. And they all agreed, except Billy said daily.

And I was called up to the parlour again, and Mr E apologized to me, all sobbing and teary, but I could see in his eye he hates me worse than ever. But he will not dare do it again, so that is something, I suppose.

Still crying myself, with anger as well as fright. That evil boy!

Wednesday, 5th March

Did not go to the Crystal Palace with the Family. Mrs McK said, I don't think Baby should come today, Lily, it is raining. But that was not why. She is mortified, and will be looking for excuses to send me away. All the other servants is scared for me, and Angelique furious that I let out her secret.

Friday, 7th March

Feel old and weary. Not with Baby, she is lovely, always happy.

Mrs McK suspected me, even after I been 3 years with the Paxtons and 6 months with her and never stole even a lump of sugar. That hurts worst. And never apologized nor nothing.

Twice her son has near got me dismissed. And a sovereign is supposed to make it right.

Did not think as I would want to write any more in this book. But who else can I talk to? Baby?

This book has done what it was meant to, and saved someone from getting turned off. Did not think it would be me.

Monday, 10th March

Going to be a Radical like Cook, and work for reform. The gentry are rotten, even them as seem good. And if they read this I don't care.

Wednesday, 12th March

Went out with the Family to the Palace today. Baby was whiny and kept me busy. Nobody spoke to me, not even Miss L. She smiled at me when nobody was looking. Couldn't smile back.

Scaffolding everywhere for the painters. The iron is being painted in red, blue, yellow and white to give a feeling of solidity and distance, Major explained. Like being inside a decanter – dazzling, no shadows. Will be like a stove house in summer which will be trouble for the food displays, butter and that. Mackerel will stink in an hour. They are draping cotton cloth across the roof, to keep it shadier and cooler.

In the Civil Engineering section, Mr Chance who made the glass sheets is showing crystal lighthouse lenses, enormous. Master's blotting-paper sketch is hung in the Stationery Court.

The Times is saying that spies and foreigners will throw bombs when the Queen is inside, or break the glass and shoot her with pistols, or lightning will hit and explode it. There is something new every week, almost every day, and they are always blaming Prince Albert because he is foreign, but I like him. He is in every day to see it, working hard to get everything organized with Master and Mr Fox, and Mr Cole, and all the others as raised money and supported the Exhibition.

A whole locomotive engine in the Machinery area, and printing presses and a machine that sews seams, and all sorts. And the machine as the Master invented for cutting gutters for the glass, as let the building be built so fast, and looms, and all sorts of engines I don't understand. But it is an Exhibition of the Works of Industry of All Nations, so the engines of industry have to be here for them as know about them.

Easier to write about this than about the Family. Hurts less.

Saturday, 15th March

Taking Baby up from visiting her mama when Miss L beckoned me from the schoolroom door and asked, Why didn't you come for your lesson last Sunday? I did not know if I should be welcome, Miss, I said, very stiff.

Oh, Lily! she said, near crying. Please come! Don't let Edgar spoil it! You're my only friend. Then Mr E came out on to the stair and Miss L whispered, Little pig, he'd tell Mama. They don't want me to speak to you, but please come tomorrow! And then she nipped back into the schoolroom.

True enough, she has nobody, with Mrs McK not going out to meet people.

Sunday, 16th March

Went for my lesson. But Mrs McK sat with us in the schoolroom so we cannot talk openly. Today I learned et cetera.

Tuesday, 18th March

Afternoon off. Mam is angry for me, but resigned about Jake. Not me. Why should Jake die, as is good and hard-working and honest etc., when that evil little monster is healthy? But God says, The wicked flourish like the green bay tree. He will get his come-uppance in God's good time. May I be there to see it, amen!

Mam said I should stick with the lessons, as Miss L needs me. Odd thought.

Wednesday, 19th March

Pouring rain, drainpipes inside the pillars of the Palace are blocked, and the wet is dripping all over inside. Major says Colonel S and his friends are saying the exhibits will be ruined by the damp, or the glass will magnify the sun's rays and set everything alight. Can't make up their minds! Made me chuckle for the first time in weeks. Major noticed and frowned, upset me again.

Huge marble and bronze statues all wrapped in canvas standing outside ready to be rolled in all along the nave, 2 are Her Majesty and Prince Albert on horses, life-size. Huge gates at the north entrance, bronze over twiddly cast iron, 60 feet wide, very impressive. Hope they don't rust!

In the Canada room, canoes of birch bark, and silverware and sleighs and Indian feather bonnets. Carriages from London and Belgium and sledges from America, with velvet and fine leather upholstery. Ironware, stoves like Greek urns, an iron bedstead with angels round it, railings, lamps, a knife with 80 blades all engraved and with gold inlay. Supposed to be a pocket knife but you'd need a wheelbarrow to carry it. Stupid.

The Hindoo as came to see Mrs McK was there with Indian soldiers, more turbans and fierce moustaches and swords. Mr E was very polite, remembering the black man, I bet! The huge diamond big as my fist as came from India will be in with the Queen's jewels, guarded by British soldiers. Major says he is a Maharajah (the Hindoo) as means big king. Mary went all queer when I told her she had served tea to a king. I said, When Queen Victoria visited Chatsworth, she spoke to me and gave me a shilling, a proper British monarch, not just a heathen, so you needn't give yourself airs. She was peeved.

Saturday, 22nd March

Advertisement in newspapers for printed engravings of Master, by permission of the Duke of Devonshire, up to 2 guineas each! Also pictures of Prince Albert and the Palace, and piano music, 12 Crystal Palace Polkas for 2/-, and maps, one on a glove as you can wear and look at as you walk, and mugs with pictures printed on, and tins of sweets and soap boxes and all sorts of souvenirs, they call them. London is going crazy about the Exhibition.

Sunday, 23rd March

Learned about putting commas round spoken words. Baby has colic.

Wednesday, 26th March

One of the rooms is called Roman Court. Statues all round dark red walls, and models of buildings of Rome but cut and opened so you can see all round inside. Mediaeval Court, with carved wood and gilt and paintings and stained glass, like Count Orlando the Vampire. Much more interesting. Freddy, Jake's friend, was helping set up stands for books from Switzerland. He gave me a grin, and Miss L waggled her fingers at him secretly, twinkling, till Mr E said loudly, "Look, Mama, one of the boys we met while we were out with Lily." Major glared. They are very careful of her now, to keep her away from the lower classes, even Freddy who saved her.

The Duke of Wellington stopped to talk to the Major.

He pinched my bum. Right through my coat and dress and 3 petticoats. Naughty old man! But I didn't make a fuss. Mr E saw, and tried it himself, so I stepped back and trod on his toe, hard. The Duke and England's Hero is one thing, but a nasty little boy is a b***** insult.

Post Office installed inside the Palace as people will want to send letters postmarked from there, or telegrams. And a big tent at one end, for ovens and tables, to feed the crowds. Outside, of course.

Sunday, 30th March

Learned about them high-up commas for who owns something. Went back and put them in. Hope I got it right.

Tuesday, 1st April

Mr E is in prison, for trying to put me there. I knew God would catch up with him.

Went to the Palace, into the room with all the fine clocks.

Freddy was in there, helping install cases again. Gave me a wink. Duke of Wellington came in again, in a plain black coat as usual, tall and white-haired and striking, though old. He saw me keeping clear, right by the door and facing him all the time, and grinned and laughed like a donkey braying, as he does, "Haw, haw!"

He started to explain a naval clock to Mr E and Miss L, how it helped sailors find their way across the ocean, and gave her his watch – a big gold half-hunter engraved all over – so they could compare them. Then he called the exhibitor to explain the mathematics. Mr E fidgeted all over the room, not paying no attention. Then the Duke said, "My watch, if you please, Miss Laura." So she turned to a case and said, "Just here, Your Grace."

But it wasn't.

Horrible pause. Then the Duke said, quite calm, "Has anyone left the room in the last few minutes?" "No, Sir," I said, nervous. "No one has passed me." So the Duke said, "Then it must still be in here. Major, call the Guards." Major stuck out his head, and called, and 4 soldiers in red coats trotted up. And the Duke said, "No one may leave. We must search everyone."

"Oh, surely not the ladies!" Mrs McK flustered, but Miss L said firmly, "Yes, Mama, certainly! I deeply apologize, Your Grace, for my carelessness."

The Duke frowned down at her, I could see why his soldiers

were in such awe of him. He said, "Miss Laura, if you were one of my soldiers I'd have you court-martialled and shot! But as you are not, you can give me a kiss and I'll forgive you – as long as we find my watch!"

They called in a friend of the Duke, an elderly lady, brisk and practical, who ordered a curtain set up across a corner for privacy. "Please search me first!" said Miss L. Mrs McK, all upset and quivery, told me, "Lily, you go in with Miss Laura." And when we came out, Mrs McK went in, and another lady who had been there. The soldiers searched Freddy and the workmen putting up the cases and finishing them off, and then the exhibitors who were there, and then Mr E, and suddenly one of them grunted, "Got it! In his pocket, Sir!" And he held up the watch in triumph.

"No, no! It wasn't me!" Mr E screamed.

Mrs McK fainted.

The lady who had searched us rubbed Mrs McK's hands and sent for water and brought her to herself, and got her sitting on a wheelbarrow with her head down, sobbing but quiet. But I was not paying that much attention, because Miss L had cried, "Edgar! You wanted to make us blame Lily again, you little snake!" "Be silent, Laura!" her papa shouted, but the Duke raised a hand to stop him. "No, Major," he said. "I want to hear this."

So Miss L, in a fury, told His Grace all about what Mr E had done with the brooch, and his face grew grimmer and grimmer.

Major turned almost green behind his moustache, and sat down beside his wife as if his legs would not hold him. Freddy got him a drink of water too.

All this time Mr E was snivelling and protesting, "No, I didn't touch it!"

When Miss L finished, "And no doubt he'd have hidden the watch, perhaps among the baby's wraps, to incriminate Lily," the Duke looked down his hooky nose at Mr E as if he was a bit of dog dirt on his shoe, and then at the Major the same way, and asked, "Is this correct, Sir?"

Somehow the Major struggled up to his feet, and bowed. "Yes, Sir," he said stiffly as Mrs McK wailed again. "I fear I have failed in my duty to the boy," he went on. "I can claim no special privilege for him because of my rank or wounds in Her Majesty's service." Trying to, underneath the words, see? Though at least he was honest and didn't try to lie.

The Duke just looked at him with contempt and said, "No." Then he nodded to the Guards. "Deliver the brat to the policemen at the nearest Court. The magistrates may apply to me at 3 this afternoon for my statement." He tucked his watch away in its pocket and stalked out.

The soldiers dragged Mr E out, screeching to his mama. She tried to go after him, screaming, "Major McKenzie, he is your son, your only living son, save him, oh God, save him!" like in a novel. But the Major held her back. "I'll telegraph to Barbrook from here, yes, and then go after Edgar,

Mrs McKenzie," he said, tugging at his moustache. "Laura, take your mama home." He was almost frantic with shame and worry as he left.

Freddy got us a cab to Charles Street. Mrs R was out, but Angelique ran out and Mary, and helped Mrs McK to bed. Miss L went right to her room and cried for hours. I nipped down to the servants' hall and told Mr B and the rest what had happened.

"They might just transport Mr E to Australia," Cook suggested, "him being so young."

She wanted to say, "Serves him right!" But seeing the suffering of his family, none of us could be so cruel, except Billy who cheered. Not even me, and it was me he was trying to get hanged.

Wednesday, 2nd April

Nothing in the newspapers about Mr E. Mr B told us all at luncheon, "We shall not talk to the press. It is our duty to protect our employers," and he frowned special hard at Billy and Hannah in case they hoped to earn a few shillings for telling tales. But it does nobody no good to be connected with dishonesty.

Mrs R thinks so. She had Angelique packing all night, ready to leave this morning, and bumped right into Master and Madam as they arrived. "You are leaving, Virginia?" Madam asked. Mrs R looked defiant. "I must consider my husband's reputation, Sarah," she said. Madam just looked at her, the same way the Duke looked at Mr E yesterday. "I always knew you were selfish, with no family loyalty, Virginia," she said, cold as ice. They never did like each other much. So Mrs R stormed off, and Madam went up to Mrs McK.

I was on the stairs and stood back on the landing to let Madam pass. She paused and sighed. "You do seem to draw trouble to this family, Lily," she said. "I know this was not your doing – none of it is! But. . ." She shook her head and went on up. I shall be dismissed yet, I am sure of it, for what is not my fault. Surprised I lasted this long.

Ran down to listen with Mr B by the parlour door. He didn't chase me, he was earwigging too. Major is punishing the brandy – 3 bottles since yesterday – and didn't even say good morning. "He's ruined me, Joseph," he shouted, "I'll have to resign. I'll always be known as the man whose son tried to rob the Duke of Wellington. God damn the little monster, I wish he had died with the others!" We had all been feeling sorry for him, a little waffly man hiding behind a big moustache, but at that, Mr B whispered, "Unnatural father!"

Master thought the same. We are afraid he will be disgraced as well, him and Mr E being related, but he did not mention it. "How is he, Jonathan? You have hired him a comfortable cell and are taking his food in?" "Certainly," said the Major. Mr B blinked, first we had heard of it. Master asked, "Is there no doubt? Does he admit it?"

"Cowardly, lying little swine!" Major snarled. "I should have sent him home to school when he was 5!" He went ranting on about Indian servants and useless women having no idea of proper discipline, till we had to jump away as Mrs McK came running down in her wrapper crying, "Joseph, Joseph, you must save him! You are a great man, you have the Queen's ear! Bring my darling back to me!" Madam hurried down after her, I just nipped in the servants' door out of sight in time. Mr B didn't wait to be asked but took in the brandy.

Went back to the nursery, and sure enough, Master came upstairs and spoke to me, and sent Mrs C for Miss L and spoke to her, where he was sure he wouldn't be interrupted. And then shook his head and looked grim, and left.

Madam is having a hard time comforting Mrs McK, who just weeps and wails all day. Major got drunk again. Baby is fretful, and I don't blame the mite, it is affecting us all.

Thursday, 3rd April

This afternoon Miss L came into the nursery while I was bathing Baby. She looked sad, flumped down on a chair and sent Mrs C out for a cup of tea. Mrs C was unwilling for the first time ever, she was dying to hear what Miss L wanted.

Soon as she was gone, "I can hardly believe this, Lily," Miss L said. "I never liked Edgar much. Indian servants always make so much more of a boy than a girl, and so did Papa, when he bothered with us at all. And Mama was always prostrated by the heat, or nursing, or in mourning. Do you know, many mothers in India don't mourn for a child who dies, it happens so often? But Mama did, and seldom had time for the rest of us. Edgar was always spoiled and selfish and malicious. As we both know!" She smiled a little, trying to act normal. "But even so, it was such a silly thing for him to do! How could he have thought he'd get away with it?"

I sniffed. "You mean you'd have accused him if the watch had been found on me, Miss Laura?" I said. "Your own brother? In front of all them important people?"

"All *those* important people, Lily," she said absently, teaching me even then, ever so precise-spoken and clever she is, "and yes, of course I should have spoken out! One must do what is right!"

I looked disbelieving, couldn't help it. Her lip trembled and she stiffened and went off hurt. But I don't know if she would have had the courage. Not really.

I was sorry I added to her sadness. She has been good to me, not meaning to get me into trouble, and I have her lily painting on the wall above my bed in the nursery corner. I feel sick.

Friday, 4th April

Madam is running the household again. Mrs McK was just waving her hand and crying, "Don't bother me, do what you like!" Cook is relieved to be told what meals to serve. Mr B and me, that Madam trained, we go on properly, but Mary needs to be pushed and watched, and Peggy is willing but still needs training.

Major was too drunk to come to dinner tonight again, and Mrs McK has a tray in her room. She and Madam go in to see Mr E every afternoon, with meals in a basket, and she comes back weeping and helpless. So just Madam and Miss L at dinner, and scarcely a word spoken, Mary says.

Mr E will come up for trial next week. I will be called as a witness.

It is all dreadful.

Tuesday, 8th April

Don't know if I am on my head or my heels.

Mam came this morning, and Mr B sent Billy up to fetch me down to speak to her. She said Jake was desperate to see me and Miss L on a matter of great importance to the Family, though he'd not say what. So I asked Mr B to speak to Madam to ask permission, and he went up to the parlour while Cook told Hannah to make Mam some tea. But Madam said no, not unless Mam could explain why it was so important.

Mam was frantic. "Wouldn't tell me, not no way, but he says as you must come, you must, right away."

"I'll ask Madam if I can take my day off next week instead of the week after," I said. "Oh, Lily, he might not be here," she said, "he's that weak, but determined he is that he must and will see you! Both of you, but even you would do – can't you come now?" "No, Mam, I can't," I said, though it nearly broke my heart, and she went off crying. Ran back up to the nursery near crying myself.

Got Baby ready to go out for her walk, telling myself all the time that I mustn't run home, no I mustn't, however much I wanted to.

Then Mrs Coppy said, "I'll look after Babby fer yer, Lily lass, if yer wants ter risk slippin' off 'ome. She's due weaned soon, so even if I'm sacked it won't make that much matter, an' worth it ter 'elp you like you 'elped me."

I was hesitating, when Miss L came in in a plain coat and bonnet. She looked, considering, at me and Baby all dressed, and at Mrs C pinning on her bonnet, and asked, "How long do you normally walk Victoria for, Lily?" "About an hour," I said, wondering. Calm and cool as Master, "And Mrs Coppy is going out with you today?" she said. "Do we have the same idea? Mrs Coppy will take care of the baby while you and I go to see Jake?"

Gobsmacked I was. But Mrs C nodded, and swore, "Swelp me, Miss, Babby'll be safer nor in the bank!"

Miss L smiled, all gracious. "Thank you, Mrs Coppy," she said. She acts like she is 20, not 14. "We shall take a hackney, and should be back in under an hour. We shall meet you by the fountain. If all goes well, no one need know that we have been away." I hesitated, and she raised an eyebrow, quite the little lady. "Well? Your mama insisted that this was vital." Mrs C was nodding, encouraging.

I gritted my teeth. "Yes, Miss, I shouldn't but I'll do it. My brother as is dying thinks it's important – and if I'm dismissed I'll not give tuppence!"

"I can understand that, Lily," she said, soft but stern. "That is why I am doing this. You know it is not easy to go against my aunt." I could only nod. She would not let me thank her, she just hurried us out.

Jake was thin, his eyes sunk in holes in his head. His face was white but with bright red cheeks, same as Dad was near the end. We knelt down by the bed to hear him whisper, because if he spoke up he coughed blood. Davy was snivelling, and Mam told Betsy to take him out and give us some peace. Then Jake said, " 'Tweren't your Edgar as took the Dook's watch. 'Twere Freddy."

Miss L gasped. "How do you know?" I asked. "He told me," Jake whispered. "He nipped it when you was all lookin' at the clocks. He were bein' sent on errands regular, fer tools or tea or that, an' he thought as he could run with it next time he were out. But then you raised the alarm, Miss, so he was stuck with it. An' he slipped it in the lad's pocket, acos he thought as a young nob wouldn't never be suspected."

"We must tell the magistrate at once!" Miss L gulped, trying to calm herself.

"No," Jake said.

"Why not?" she demanded. "Edgar is going to be hanged!"

"Freddy done it for me, an' Mam as looked after him the last 3 year. He'd get about £10 for the ticker. Half the money'd pay Mam's debts, an' for my funeral, an' the other half set up a stall for hisself, acos he couldn't go back to Smee's. So you'll not jail an' hang him to save yer brother, I won't let yer."

"Well, why did you send for us, then?" Miss L cried, desperate.

"Got an idea," he said. "Duke never noticed Freddy. I'll say as I felt better that day an' come in to work, and it were me in the Crystal Palace. Nobody'll bother to check wi' Smee's. I'll say as I took the watch, but now I'm mortal bad, an' I don't want to go wi' this on me conscience, so I'm confessin'. An' the beak'll arrest me, an' let yer brother out o' jail. An' Freddy'll be safe too. An' I'm dyin' anyway," Jake whispered. "Jack Ketch the hangman'll have to move hisself to get his hands on me!" And he laughed, dry and papery. Lying there, like a corpse already, he laughed.

"Oh, Jake, Jake," Mam sighed. I was too dumbfounded to speak. Miss L said, "But why will you do this for us?"

Jake laughed again, and coughed up some blood. Mam wiped it away. "Not for you, Miss," he murmured. "For money. Enough to buy a cottage an' land to keep Mam an' the little uns, an' a bit put away for a cold winter. You gimme that, an' I'll see yer right. But if yer don't, I'll not."

"I could tell the magistrate what you've said," said Miss L. Jake's lips twitched. "Hearsay evidence, Miss, not good enough, not when Lily an' Mam an' me, we all say as you made it up to save yer brother."

She turned to me, quite shocked. "Lily? Would you

really lie, and let Edgar be punished for something he didn't do?"

Mam looked worried. I sighed. "Easy to be honest, Miss, when you've got food and money and a pleasant life. To get Mam out of here I'd do worse than lie, God forgive me. But it's Jake will be lying, aye, and maybe dying, for your brother." I looked her right in the eye. "Well, Miss?"

She took a deep breath, same as me earlier, and said, "Yes! I'll arrange it. Papa brought back a lot of jewels and gold from India, loot from a palace, he said. He can use some of that to pay you. How much do you want? Would £100 be enough?" Jake nodded.

And then Master walked in.

Never saw him in such a rage. Brigade of Guards would've run away. He stood and glared, cold and hard, at me and Miss L who had come to this place where Miss L had been attacked before, where she had been absolutely forbidden to come again. Mam squeaked. My insides shrank up into a hurtful knot. Even Miss L knelt silent by the bed.

It was Jake broke the silence. "Mr Paxton," he said, with the hint of a smile. "Come in, Sir. Yer welcome."

"My wife met Mrs Coppy in the park, Laura." Mrs C couldn't have kept the secret, not against Madam. "The woman is packing her things now, and Mrs Paxton has told me to dismiss Lily forthwith."

I never respected Miss L more than that minute. For she

118

stood up and said, almost calmly, "Uncle Joseph, they acted on my instructions. If they are dismissed I shall myself pay them another 4 weeks' wages and give them a character reference. But I hope Aunt Sarah will change her mind when she hears why we disobeyed Papa. Pray listen to me, Uncle Joseph, because this is immensely important."

Never respected Master more than then, neither, when he held back his anger like a driver reining a hard-mouthed horse, and listened to Miss L carefully, glancing down at Jake as if he couldn't believe it. And Jake just lay and grinned like a skeleton.

And we all waited.

Master said, "Blame a boy, a sick boy, who is innocent, and allow the guilty party to walk free? Certainly not!"

"But Sir, it's your own nephew! Don't you care for him?" I almost shouted. Should have known better. "You are suggesting that I should commit a deception, in sheer dishonesty, to benefit my own family?" he snapped.

But Miss L stood up to him for me. "Lily is quite right, Uncle Joseph. Strict righteousness here will be worse than useless, for we have no evidence. To accuse this Freddy, lacking any proof or supporting statements—" she looked at me and Jake, and we both nodded, though I was near too scared to move, "will make you look a fool, ruin our family, cause Edgar's death, Papa's disgrace, Mama's nervous collapse. How is this preferable to a white lie, practical and generous, done in kindness and love, which will harm no one but bring happiness to us all?"

"A lie is a lie. This is mere emotional female quibbling—" Master said, and Miss L interrupted, as I'd never have dared, "And is it the worse for being a woman's argument, Sir? Are emotions always irrelevant? Your original design for the exhibition hall was for a single straight hall, yet when the protests about cutting down those trees forced you to add the arched transept, you said it improved the whole design. And that was emotional."

Master stopped short. At last, after about 10 years it seemed like, he said, "You have a point, Laura." Almost surprised at himself. "Yet it is still dishonest."

"Dishonest?" Miss L exclaimed. "Uncle Joseph, you constantly stress the importance of a sense of proportion in your work. Pray use it now." I hoped she knew what she was talking about, I didn't, but she always was cleverer than me. "No one raises an eyebrow at Papa's stealing gold and jewels from a Sikh king's palace. Even the great diamond, the Koh-i-noor, was taken from India by force, yet the Queen accepted it, and it will be on display in your Crystal Palace. Will you object to that, which is flatly theft? Then is it not pure hypocrisy to quibble at this minor deceit? Which is the worse crime?"

And he looked at her, standing determined and steadfast there, more adult than her mama, and at Jake in the huddle of blankets, and said, "Dammit, Laura, you're more my child than any of my children. Yes, yes, very well." We all let out a breath we didn't know we was holding.

And then I made myself speak. "Sir? Sir, I got something to ask. To beg you. Don't let the household know it was Jake. I'd never hear the end of it – my brother a thief. . ." I had to stop, but he was nodding thoughtfully.

"True, Lily. I appreciate your problem. The other servants, and also," he added, deadly serious, "Mrs Paxton, and Edgar's mother, must never hear the true story. We declare that the urgent message was that Jake here had discovered the thief – which is not a lie – but we do not need to name the culprit. I disapprove of children keeping secrets from their parents, but in this case—"

"I do understand, Sir," Miss L said. Right enough, Mistress has rigid principles, she'd never agree, and Mrs McK would blab it all over London. "Nor shall I tell Edgar."

He glanced at me, stern and severe, not wanting the word to get out that he'd compromised with his conscience, and who'd blame him, but it suited me. "Thank you, Sir! Silent as the grave, Sir," I promised, and blushed, but Jake just grinned again.

Master nodded, and turned to Jake. "£100? Nonsense. Jonathan can well afford £200. Little enough for his son's life."

"Less £20, pay yer back me 'prentice fee, Sir," Jake husked. "An' today. Might not be here tomorrow!"

Miss L and Mam and me winced, but, "Quite right,

young man," Master said calmly. "The Major will go with you to the bank this afternoon, and set up an account for you, Mrs Hicks."

Mam looked alarmed. "I never been in a bank, Sir, I couldn't!"

"Let Lily go," suggested Miss L, and Mam nodded, grateful. "That's better, Miss, an' I'll get Jake ready." She was near crying, but he reached for her hand and said, "Mam, I promised Dad I'd look after you, an' this is the best I can do."

We left her hugging him, and went home. Mrs C had gone, and Madam wanted me dismissed also, but when we told them the tale we had agreed on, Mrs McK wouldn't hear of it. "Dismiss the sister of my son's saviour? Never, Sarah, never!" she almost screamed, and Madam could only shrug.

So after luncheon, when I had settled Baby with her mama, I went with Master and the Major to the bank. First time for me too, I was scared stiff. Biggest house I've seen, except for Chatsworth, all brown marble columns, but the bank gents very respectful even to me. They set up an account for Mam there, in her name and mine so I could get money out for her. £200. A fortune. Master dismissed the idea of paying back the £20. "Don't insult me, Lily!"

Then we went back to Mam's. Major was stiff and awkward, not knowing what to say, but Master was kindness itself. "My cousin and I can never thank you enough, Jake," he said, "and you, Mrs Hicks." He shook Jake's hand, and looked at the Major until he did the same, and carried Jake down his own self to the cab.

By the time I calmed Mam down, and showed her the bank book, and calmed her down again, and walked back to Charles Street, Mr E was home already, ever so quiet. Mrs McK was weeping again, and wanting to kiss me out of gratitude, and saying she must visit my brother as saved her boy (as near gave me a fit, and set the Master coughing over his cigar, but I said Jake was too ill and he shut his eyes and sighed quiet-like with relief) and the Major harrumphing, and Miss L looking as if she saw angels, and Madam smiling but disapproving, especially of me. And all the other servants near busting with curiosity.

So I escaped to the nursery again. I was crying too. For Jake.

Nearly 4 in the morning, but I cannot sleep, not with all the excitement and grief and happiness, so I have just written it all out, more than ever before. My hand is aching and my fingers black with ink.

Wednesday, 9th April

Mam came in again this morning. She went to the jail last night, and found Jake in the comfortable private cell hired for Mr E, and coughing dreadful. Stayed with him so long the gates were shut on her, keeping her in. "I didn't care, Lily, Betsy could see to Ben an' Davy. An' just after midnight, Lily," she said, "Jake smiles at me, ever so sweet, an' whispers, 'I looked after you, Mam!' An' he just fell asleep, Lily, so quiet I never knew he were gone." She weren't crying nor nothing, just relieved that Jake was at rest, and the pain over.

So am I. Feel ever so sad, but he did what he wanted to in the end. Just wish it hadn't happened. I loved him.

She wants to give him a slap-up funeral – horse-drawn hearse and paid mutes to walk behind with her and weep and wail, lilies and plumes, feast for the neighbours, marble angel tombstone – but I told her no, just mourning blacks for her and the children, and a simple funeral, I'd not take more than £5 out of the bank for her, my year's wage and plenty. She called me unnatural and ungrateful, not to show proper respect to my brother, but I know I'm right. She'd spend the lot on gold coffin handles if I let her, Jake would be furious.

Thursday, 10th April

Mrs McK asked again for me to come to India with her, 19th May. Mr E is going to Winchester school, and staying with

Master and Madam in the holidays, as Miss L will do for the next 4 or 5 years till she is a proper young lady. So he would not bother me. He is very subdued since Master spoke to him to make him realize it was his own past badness made us all think he was guilty. Maybe it has been a real lesson to him.

The Family went out to the Crystal Palace today. Madam insisted, to put a stop to any rumours. But she did not ask me to go, not with Jake's dying and all. Miss L says that they are wheeling in the statues along the nave, and the painters hanging over it all finishing off, and drips of paint falling on the flags and curtains and marble. They are building a platform for the Queen's chair when she comes to open the Palace, with a canopy over it. "To keep the paint off?" I said, and she laughed. "Or the birds!" she said, free and easy and happy again.

Saturday, 12th April

Mam has started popping in every day for a few minutes, very respectful to Cook and Mr B, and gets a cup of tea and welcome because we helped the Family. She has moved already, to a clean, respectable lodging. Ordered a gravestone – couldn't stop her – black granite, ever so sombre and tasteful, inscribed for Dad and Jake and room for the rest of us below when God wills.

Monday, 14th April

Miss L came to Jake's funeral, at St Mark's, just her and me and Mam and the children (who behaved very quiet and reverential) and Mr Dodds, Jake's foreman. Not Freddy, couldn't get time off. Horse hearse and a growler to impress Mam's new neighbours, and a lovely wreath of hot-house lilies, and a meal at a chop-house, 8d each, all except Mr Dodds, he had to get back to French polish the furniture for the Crystal Palace.

Miss L very impressed. "English funerals are very solemn and dignified, Lily." Depends where you are, and who. Dad had a pauper's funeral, handcart and coffin hired from the parish, and him laid in a common grave with a dozen more, and all his mates fighting drunk. Solemn and dignified, huh!

Tuesday, 15th April

Colonel S is going his duster again in The Times, that the salute of guns to mark the opening will shatter the glass and cut the ladies all to mincemeat. "The gents can look after theirselves," Cook said, laughing. Some people believe it, though. Troops ready in London to protect the Queen, peelers won't be enough to control the crowds and put down the riots Colonel S says always happen when working people gather together. Nonsense. Not even smoking allowed, nor drink nor foul language on pain of arrest, nor dogs, and it's to be shut on Sundays to respect the Sabbath Day. You'd get more riots in a Sunday School. Pompous old goat.

Definitely becoming a Radical.

Baby has cut her 1st tooth. If I don't go to India, I'll lose her.

Wednesday, 16th April

Duke of Wellington there again, came over and spoke to Major stiff but polite. Major said after, "He will put in a good word for me when I return to India. I may even hope for promotion." Beamed at Mr E as if the boy had done him a good turn. Mr E very subdued these days. Could even wish he was a bit more lively – never thought I'd say that!

The Crystal Palace is more wonderful every time we go, with coloured light everywhere, so airy and delicate, but strong. Not like a house, solid and heavy and shadowy, solid to the ground. Like being inside a diamond it is, or a fairy palace. Master has made a miracle, everybody says so. And inside, there's more and more exhibits every day, 10,000 they say. We saw French and Belgian lace and English embroidery today, so fine the Queen can't have better – shawls and baby gowns and waistcoats, and Irish double damask tablecloths with shimmering ferns and flowers woven in. I was near crying with pure delight it was all so lovely.

Tickets are dear, 1/- during the week, 2/6 on Fridays, 5/- Saturdays. There's reduced rates for schools and groups from Workmen's Institutes, as is very good, but season tickets is 5 guineas, my yearly wage! So much to see, though, it is worth every penny. Glad I could come for free, all the same!

Friday, 18th April

Master asked to see Mam and me in his office. Worried me, but he was smiling. "Mrs Hicks," he said, "in the bank, your money will earn you £8 a year, less this tiresome income tax of about 1/- in the pound. Not a great deal." Mam and me looked shocked, we thought £200 was a fortune. "A cottage and land will cost £100 or so, which will make it even less. I believe you could do better."

"Yes, sir?" said Mam, hopeful.

"A Mr Thomas Cook is organizing cheap excursions for associations of working men and their families from all over the country, with return tickets to London at a single fare for parties of 200 or more. Lodging-houses at 1/- or 2/- a night, and good meals at 6d or a shilling, are being set up for the expected crowds, some with separate dormitories for men and women. Decent women are needed to superintend the women's rooms." He looked with approval at her new respectable blacks. "If you wish, I can recommend you to the owner of the Clarence Club House. You would have a room and board for yourself and your children and also a wage of 8/- weekly. Would you. . .?"

Mam was gasping, "Oh, yes, Sir, if you please!"

Master was smiling – he does like to arrange things to suit people. "Later, if you find the work agreeable, you might make a good living as a hotel-keeper, with the help of your family."

He brushed aside Mam's thanks and questions, saying, "Come along, I shall take you to meet the owner at once." So Mam went off with him, all excited.

Think it was Madam who suggested the hotel idea to him, meaning for me to join Mam and all, not just the little ones, to get me away from the Family before I cause more trouble.

Sunday, 20th April

Miss L has me reading books to her, and explains as we go, so I learn new words every week. Though I do not know what good the history of Rome will do me.

Wednesday, 23rd April

The Crystal Palace is humming, noisy, echoing with workmen doing last-minute things – altering cases, mending torn hangings, fitting curtains and painting over scratches – and artists drawing the exhibits to make engravings for the catalogue. Rubbish everywhere.

Prince Albert was there again, ever so handsome. The Queen comes often too, but not the same times as we.

Porters dropped a huge, heavy piano from New York, all carved rosewood, right in front of the Commissioner for America. A leg was broke (on the piano, not him). Mr Dodds as was delivering Mr Smee's bed and cabinet, offered to repair it. So saw Freddy again, helping with tools and glue. He winked, a bit shamefaced, but he only wanted to help. So I winked back, and he grinned like a slice of melon. Mr Smee's bed is decorated every inch with carving, and crimson silk curtains, very rich. Miss L admired the vases of flowers in fine wood marquetry that Jake cut the veneers for, on the sideboard, and Mr E bit his lip.

Pianos everywhere, and beds, and naked statues. One bed very gothic, from Vienna, carved with Adam and Eve, and finished with more red brocade and gold fringes. And one in the Belgian room, with naked ladies carved in ebony with gilt twiddly bits. Mrs McK hurried Miss L and I past smartish but Major twirled his moustache and said, "It's art, my dear." Maybe, but popular, I'll bet. Specially with the Duke of Wellington. Maybe that's why he comes so often.

Friday, 25th April

Mr E came to me, all on his own, shaky but determined, and apologized for giving me so much trouble. And then he went downstairs and promised them to behave well in future, too. Mary is charmed, but Cook says she'll believe it if it lasts.

Miss L came into the nursery, and said, "Lily, please go with Mama to India. Please, she needs you!" True enough, she does – she is all weepy and clinging – and so does Baby. So I said yes. She kissed me, all delighted.

So it is settled. Mam is happy in her new job. The children are going to school, and working at the lodging-house before and after it. Ben is the Boots like Billy here, and Betsy is helping the maids, and even Davy earns more from tips than Ben did at the bakehouse – what with workmen bringing their families to see the Crystal Palace before they have to buy a ticket when it opens proper – and they all are better fed than for years. Mam says hotel-keeping is no harder than running a house of your own, and she can manage fine without me. So it is all settled, and everybody pleased.

But I shall never be Housekeeper at Chatsworth now.

Monday, 28th April

The Crystal Palace will be opened in 3 days, so the Family went to see it one last time. I did not go. Cook found me a book about India, warning to boil every drop of water for half an hour. Scary. Mrs McK has 14 new dresses to wrap in lead foil so they will keep dry in trunks in the ship's hold, and lots of books and music – Crystal Palace Polkas! And 2 cabin trunks for clothes for the voyage.

Mr B is going as second butler to Lord Granville's town house, all puffed up like a bullfrog, a good step up for a young man. Cook went to the employment agency, says she has her pick of 4 positions, and will interview the ladies next week! Mary says she will get married, she wants a house of her own instead of staying in service. Peggy and Hannah will go to Madam at Barbrook. Billy will go and help Davy. So we are all settled.

I do not need to keep this journal any more. It is almost full, too. But I shall write it until I leave for India, and then like as not start another.

Tuesday, 29th April

Master at the Crystal Palace most of the day. The Queen was there too, and most gracious. The last workmen are finishing off – carpet fitters and upholsterers and seamstresses doing last alterations and mending. Tonight the soldiers will clear everybody out, and tomorrow it will all be cleaned, swept out, dusted and polished, and the glass washed ready for Thursday.

Town is full of people. 1,000s come for the opening. 10s of 1,000s. 100s of 1,000s!

Found Mary crying, hiding in a cupboard. None of her followers wants to marry her. Achitophel has another girl that she did not know about, and the Corporal ran away when she hinted she would accept an offer, and Walter is getting engaged to a grocer's daughter with 4 shops. So Mary is left alone, after all her flirting. Promised I'd not tell the others, they would jeer, especially Billy.

Wednesday, 30th April

Miss L is a sly-boots! She came into the nursery just when I had taken Baby in to her mama for the afternoon rest, and said, "Lily, this letter has come for Uncle Joseph, marked 'Urgent'. He's at the Crystal Palace, supervising the last details. Come along, we'll take it to him, and see it all ready for the Queen!" So we did. Just as well we had gone so often, the Guards knew Miss L and let us in when she smiled and charmed them. Wish I could do it.

Lord Grafton was with Master, laughing, and saying, "I promised you, Paxton. I'm told the Lord Chamberlain has the sword all ready for you!" Worried me, but Miss L was hissing with excitement. But she shushed me when I asked what it meant, and went up to them quite calm.

Master laughed too when he saw us, and said, "Ah, Laura! I might have known you would find a way to see the final result!" Lord Grafton took Miss L's arm, like a lady, and said, funning, "Allow me to escort you, Madam, to view your uncle's triumph!" And he walked her in to show her round, so I just followed on.

Magical. All the mess was cleared away, and there was

men arranging banks of flowers, and seats all down the aisles. The light and colours are like fairyland. The crystal fountain was playing, as if it was special for us, and the smaller ones on too, ever so lovely. We went right along the nave, under all the statues, and Lord G took Miss L up a red carpet on to the Queen's platform where they were putting in the throne. But wouldn't let her sit on it! They were trying the huge organ – lovely music echoing in that vast space, so light and airy, like heaven.

Exhibits still coming in! The catalogue will not be complete till tonight. Then printing machines inside the Palace will print 1,000s ready for tomorrow, and bookbinders will work all night to finish the first 2 in morocco leather and gold leaf trimming for the Queen and Prince Albert.

When we left, Miss L explained what Lord G had meant about the sword. It is decided, Master is really going to be made a knight! He is also to get the medal for the best exhibit of all, the Crystal Palace itself! When I told them all downstairs, Mr B nipped another bottle of port for us.

Thursday, 1st May

Master off early to the Crystal Palace. He'd be inside with the Commission and Mr Cole and the rest who had had the 1st idea and worked so hard to make it happen. Only season ticket holders are allowed there today. Prince Albert had ticket number 1 and the Queen doesn't need one, of course!

Family went to see the procession from a friend's window. As they was away all day they didn't take Baby. Mrs McK said I could leave her with Peggy for an hour, to let me and Mary go out to see the Opening. Ever so considerate. Mr B said we could not go without an escort, so he came too. Cook stayed in, said it was all nonsense. I think she disapproves of the Royal Family and might be a Republican which is even worse than a Radical. With no luncheon to make she said she'd look after Baby so Peggy could get out too, and she let Billy and Hannah go out, but like as not they'd have run off anyway.

Mary and Peggy and I didn't see much, we were too late out. Hundreds had been sleeping in the park even in the rain to get a good place. Never saw such crowds, with people climbing on walls and trees and roofs, and boys up on gas standards, and everybody jammed till you could scarcely move or breathe. Guards was lining the road to Buckingham Palace to keep it clear.

Peggy had her pocket picked, but only a handkerchief. We helped a woman who was fainting and would have been trampled on – got her into the eating tent where she could sit down. People squeezed up to let us by – Mr B is stronger than he looks and we were glad of him. It was lucky for we got nearer the Crystal Palace than we could on our own. Everyone was happy and joyful, out for a good time, and there wasn't no trouble nowhere.

"O look, in among the nobs!" Mary said. "A Chinaman! Must be a Mandarin!" "No, he's just the captain of a scruffy little ship," I told her, "Miss Laura and I met him near Mam's once." We had a good laugh at the gentry all bowing back to him.

A regimental band on the lawn. I could just see the red coats and the Queen's white dress and the sparkle of her coronet. A ray of sunlight made the whole hall shine like diamonds just as her carriage arrived and the guns that welcomed her didn't shatter the glass. Cheering to deafen you. When she went in we couldn't hear the speeches, but could just hear the music, choirs and the American organ, and we all sang the National Anthem with them, and then Mr Handel's Hallelujah Chorus, and then the National Anthem again, and trumpets, and the Queen drove back to wave to the crowd from the balcony at Buckingham Palace.

Such a celebration, with laughing and gaiety and joking, all joyous like being in church. My heart was soaring like angels, I shall never ever forget it!

We were out nearly 4 hours, not 1, never noticed the time. My throat was sore with singing and cheering. Mrs McK will never know, Baby was fine with Cook. Hannah and Billy were not back till 5, and Cook clipped their ears but not too hard. "Can't expect nothing else, with all these capers!"

Wonder if Colonel S is disappointed there wasn't a riot.

Friday, 2nd May

Pages and pages in The Times about the Crystal Palace, all praising – they wouldn't dare not. "Yesterday was witnessed a sight the like of which in the nature of things can never happen again... The edifice, the treasures of art, the assemblage and solemnity of the occasion ... more than sense can scan or imagination attain ... all that is beautiful in nature and art ... a glittering arch more lofty and spacious than the vaults of even our noblest Cathedrals."

Don't remember much solemnity, but I wasn't inside. The rest is true enough. I just thought it was miraculous.

They wrote about the Chinaman, too, as a "live

importation from the Celestial Empire", thinking he was an ambassador from the Emperor of China. We laughed ourselves silly.

Mrs McK has ordered me 2 new dresses, and underthings too. I can get tailors in India to copy them quick and cheap.

Saturday, 3rd May

Mam hadn't been in for a week, and I thought she must be busy, so I walked Baby out across to Clarence Club House to see her. She was coughing, and red spots in her cheeks.

Sunday, 4th May

In a way it is a relief. I can't go to India, not with Mam sick. Who would look after her, and then the children? So Mary will go in my place. Mrs McK wept, but had to accept it. Mary will work in the nursery with me till they leave, to learn how to look after Baby, and I have given her the India book. Madam and Mrs McK both gave me a good reference. I have got myself a job as parlourmaid, not in a private house, but in a hotel near Mam to learn the business.

This is the last page. I shall keep this book to remember everything.

I shall never be Housekeeper at Chatsworth, nor a Colonel's wife. But some day I will have the best hotel in London. I shall call it the Crystal Hotel, after the wonderful Crystal Palace that made it possible. And to remind me of Master and Mistress, and Jake and even Mr E, and everybody. Especially Miss L.

Funny how things change.

Historical note

By the time Victoria became queen, Britain was the world's most powerful industrial nation. In 1850, an amazing one third of the whole world's industrial output was British, and one quarter of world trade came through British ports. Britain also ruled over "colonies" in many other parts of the world, and expanded its empire as the century went on – Canada, Australia, New Zealand, Singapore, Hong Kong, India and several African countries were all part of the British Empire.

But Britain's economic success at the time came at a high price: the working people of the country (including children as young as six) worked very long hours in terrible conditions, and had no rights at all nor any say in how the Government should be run at the start of Queen Victoria's reign. The factories and mines where they worked were incredibly unhealthy and dangerous places. The towns they lived in were overcrowded and dirty: there were no proper sewers or running water, and diseases like cholera, typhoid and tuberculosis flourished in these conditions.

Working people could escape factory jobs by going into domestic service for wealthy families like the Paxtons.

Although food and living conditions could be good for servants, depending on their employers, the working day might be as long as 18 hours, and pay was terrible.

The unfairness of Victorian society was reflected in some of the novels of the time, and most famous are the ones by Charles Dickens. Dickens had known hardship himself: he worked in a factory at the age of twelve, while his father was in prison for debt. *The Pickwick Papers*, the novel being read by the servants in Lily's diary, was published in serial form in 1836.

Conditions for working people did improve gradually during the nineteenth century. A series of Factory Acts limited working hours and tried to improve conditions – the 1833 Factory Act banned children under nine from working in mills and said that children between nine and thirteen could not work for more than nine hours a day; those between thirteen and eighteen not more than twelve hours a day. (Today, normal working hours are seven hours a day for adults.) Trade Unions, which argued for the rights of workers, were first allowed to exist in the 1820s, although it wasn't common for people to belong to a Union until the beginning of the twentieth century. The Public Health Act of 1848 set up a Board of Health in London to organize proper sewers, street cleaning and pavements. In time, this led to much better sanitation and water supplies in towns. The 1832 Reform Act granted more people the vote, but it was still limited to the rich and meant that only one man in twenty could vote. Most men over 21 were given the vote by 1886, while women continued to struggle for their vote until it was granted to most women over 30 in 1918, and to all women over 21 in 1928.

Some people, of all classes, campaigned for a fairer society throughout the nineteenth century. But most accepted their position as the natural order of things, and were proud of their country's wealth and power.

The Great Exhibition of 1851 was a celebration and a symbol of Britain's success. It was called an Exhibition of the Works of Industry of All Nations, and was the world's first international exhibition (though more than half of the exhibitors were in fact British).

Henry Cole, a member of the Society of Arts, was the driving force behind the Exhibition following his visit to the Paris Exposition, a huge exhibition of French art and industry. Fired with enthusiasm, Henry Cole and Prince Albert decided to create an even better, bigger, international exhibition in London, showing works of art and industrial products. Albert saw it as "a new starting point from which all nations would be able to direct their further exertions".

Support for the scheme grew. The Government set up a Royal Commission to oversee the project, which eventually saw and approved the design by Joseph Paxton for a building to house the Exhibition – even though Paxton had drawn his design on a piece of blotting paper and had to get a complete set of plans drawn up within nine days. The site of the Exhibition was to be in London's Hyde Park, and the design had to be changed to include a domed roof so that the trees in the Park could fit inside it.

Joseph Paxton (1801–1865) worked as Head Gardener for the Duke of Devonshire and had designed the Great Conservatory at the Duke's estate at Chatsworth in 1840, but he was to become famous as the designer of the Crystal Palace which housed the Great Exhibition. His design was brilliant in its simplicity: the structure was made of prefabricated units which could be brought to Hyde Park and put together there. This meant that it could be built quickly, which was essential since time was running out. Work started in July 1850 with the Birmingham building contractors, Fox and Henderson.

The size of the building was astonishing: nothing so large had ever been built before. It was 550 metres long and 140 wide, with a ceiling 19 metres high, covering an area of 9,300 square metres – six times the size of Saint Paul's Cathedral. The frame of the building was made of cast iron, with 300,000 glass panes, like an enormous and very beautiful greenhouse – Joseph Paxton had used his experience of building conservatories and greenhouses as the basis of his design. While the structure was being built, the magazine

Punch gave it the nickname that it became known by – "The Crystal Palace".

Despite criticism, and doubts raised about the safety of the structure, the Crystal Palace was ready to be opened by Queen Victoria on 1 May 1851. Prince Albert made a speech at the opening, when he said:

> "It is our heartfelt prayer that this undertaking, which has for its end the promotion of all branches of human industry, and the strengthening of the bonds of peace and friendship among all the nations of the earth, may, by the blessing of Divine Providence, help the welfare of Your Majesty's people, and be long remembered among the brightest circumstances of Your Majesty's peaceful and happy reign."

Visitors could see 100,000 exhibits from all over the world, which included wonderful objects, from the Indian Koh-i-noor diamond, to steam hammers and printing machines, to chocolate bars (invented in 1847), to a collapsible piano for yachts. One pious lady was so shocked by the nude statues on display that she smashed some of their rude bits with her parasol!

The Great Exhibition was a huge success. Over six million people visited the Crystal Palace in the six months the Exhibition lasted. It made £200,000 profit – a vast amount then – which helped to found the Victoria and Albert Museum and Imperial College in London, and allowed several scholarships to be set up.

When the Exhibition was over, the Crystal Palace was taken down and remade in Sydenham, south of London, and opened to the public in 1854. Sadly, the Crystal Palace was badly damaged by fire in 1867 and completely burned down in 1936.

Joseph Paxton did receive his knighthood for his part in one of the most famous and memorable achievements of the Victorian age.

A note about money

Before decimalization in 1971, British currency consisted of pounds, shillings and pence. One pound was made up of 20 shillings, each containing 12 pence, making 240 pennies to the pound. The abbreviation for pennies was d and shillings was s. The symbol for pound was the same as it is today (£). You would often see prices written down separated by slashes so five shillings and six pence would be written 5/6 and just five shillings would be written 5/-.

A guinea was worth one pound and one shilling. A sovereign was worth 20 shillings and was the coin equivalent of a one pound note.

Timeline of Britain in the 1800s

1800 Act of Union creates United Kingdom of Great Britain and Ireland. King George III is on the throne. The population of Britain is about 10.5 million. (Population of Ireland is about 5.2 million.)

1802 The first in a series of Factory Acts is passed.

1807 The slave trade is banned by Britain.

1811 George III is mentally ill, so his son George acts as monarch of the country as "Prince Regent".

1815 Battle of Waterloo in which Britain and her allies defeat Napoleon – the end of long wars with France.

1819 Birth of Princess Victoria (later queen).

1820 George III dies and the Prince Regent becomes George IV.

1825 The first passenger railway is built, from Stockton to Darlington.

1829 The Metropolitan Police is formed in London by Prime Minister Robert Peel. Within the next 30 years similar forces are set up in every part of Britain.

1830 George IV dies; his brother becomes King William IV.

1832 Reform Act means that more people get the right to

vote – but it's still limited to rich men – and that areas of Britain are represented in Parliament more fairly.

1833 Slavery is abolished in Britain and all its colonies.

1837 William IV dies. Queen Victoria comes to the throne, aged 18.

1840 Victoria marries her cousin, Albert.

1842 Report by General Register Office proves that bad living conditions bring about early death.

1845 Scottish Potato Famine.

1846 Start of Irish Potato Famine, which continues until 1851. Over 1.5 million starve or emigrate.

1848 Public Health Act is passed. The Communist Manifesto by Karl Marx is published (in German), which encourages workers to organize themselves against unfair governments, though the book is not read by many ordinary people at the time.

1851 Great Exhibition in London.

1854 Crimean War (against Russia) starts and continues until 1856. Florence Nightingale begins her work as a nurse in the Crimean war hospitals.

1862 Start of American Civil War. Prince Albert dies of typhoid. Queen Victoria goes into mourning for her husband and doesn't appear in public again for 18 years.

1875 The first council houses are built, as a result of a government Act which allows local authorities to pull down slums and replace them with better housing.

1877 Queen Victoria is declared Empress of India.

1881 Married Women's Property Act allows women to keep their own property and earnings after marriage; before this everything was the property of their husbands.

1882 First Boer War (in South Africa) starts.

1886 Many British men over 21 can now vote. Women won't get the vote for another 32 years.

1891 People no longer have to pay for primary education in state schools.

1894 The first motor car is produced. The wireless is demonstrated for the first time by its inventor, Marconi.

1899 Second Boer War.

1900 The Labour Party is formed.

1901 Queen Victoria dies, aged 81, and is succeeded by her son, Edward VII. The population of Britain has now risen to about 40 million.

Joseph Paxton, designer of the Crystal Palace.

Arthur Wellesley, Duke of Wellington, in a portrait by Sir Charles Lawrence.

The Grand Entrance of the Crystal Palace showing flags of all nations flying above it.

An illustration by George Cruikshank shows vistors from all over the world flocking to see the Great Exhibition.

A crowded horse-drawn bus carries visitors to the Great Exhibition.

Glass blowers at Mr Chance's Works in Birmingham are shown making the huge panes of glass for the Crystal palace.

This picture shows glass being laid using a glazing wagon.

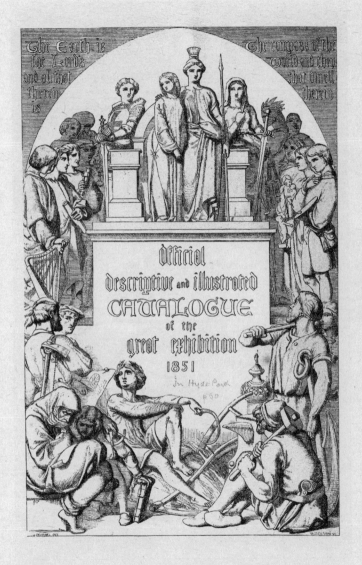

Frontispiece for the official illustrated catalogue of the Great Exhibition.

This one room, in Bethnal Green, London, was occupied by a military tailor and his large family in 1843.

Seven Dials, London, was a notorious slum area in the nineteenth century.

In the nineteenth century, upper-class children were looked after by nurse-maids and nannies rather than by their parents.

Paxton modified his design of the Crystal Palace so that the huge trees shown in this picture wouldn't have to be cut down.

Picture acknowledgments

P 152   (top left) Joseph Paxton, Popperfoto

P 152   (top right) Arthur Wellesley, Duke of Wellington, by Sir Charles Lawrence, Popperfoto

P 152   (bottom) Grand entrance to the Crystal Palace, Mary Evans Picture Library

P 153   (top) Visitors from all over the world flock to see the Crystal Palace, by George Cruikshank in *Mayhew's Great Exhibition of 1851*, Mary Evans Picture Library

P 153   (bottom) Passengers running for the bus to the Great Exhibition, by George Cruikshank in *Mayhew's Great Exhibition of 1851*, Mary Evans Picture Library

P 154   (top) Glass blowers, engraving in the *Illustrated London News*, Mary Evans Picture Library

P 154   (bottom) Using a glazing wagon, engraving in the *Illustrated London News*, Mary Evans Picture Library

P 155   Frontispiece for the Great Exhibition catalogue, Mary Evans Picture Library

P 156   Slum scene, *Illustrated London News*, Mary Evans Picture Library

P 157   (top) Dudley Street, Seven Dials, by Gustave Dore in *London, a Pilgrimage*, Mary Evans Picture Library

P 157   (bottom) A Nursemaid, by J Dinsdale in *The Girl's Own Paper*, Mary Evans Picture Library

P 158   Crystal Palace interior, engraving from a daguerreotype by Mayall, Mary Evans Picture Library

Introducing...

My Royal Story

Vividly imagined accounts of queens and
princesses from the past.

Turn the page for an exclusive extract from
'*My Royal Story: Victoria*'

1 April 1829
Kensington Palace, London, England

This book was not given to me, nor did I buy it with my own pocket money. You might say that I found it, but that would not be completely truthful. It is of a convenient small size, with many empty pages left, having only some lists of cows written in it here and there. The cover is brown, mottled paper, and someone has pasted on a white label. On the label, in very curly letters, it says *Herd Record*.

For, yes, I *stole* the book – from an out of the way, cornermost cupboard in the hall outside the harness room in the stable. I saw the cupboard swinging open once a few weeks ago, when I ducked aside to adjust my undergarments. They were binding me *mercilessly* before my excellent governess, the Baroness Lehzen, and I were to ride out in the carriage. I was itching, so Lehzen bid me go around the corner privately to compose myself and make myself presentable. (Meanwhile, she watched out for anyone who might accidentally interrupt.)

So I did, and there was a little built-in cupboard with the hook-and-eye latch undone. Inside were ledgers, twenty or so, I should say. One was lists of pigs, by name! One was carrier pigeons; one was geese and guinea fowl and such; several were sheep. None was horses – I should have preferred horses. From whose farm these records were, I know not, save, the years marked on them were between 1813 and 1815, four to six years before I was even born.

When Lehzen and I went out today, I recalled seeing the ledgers last time I was in the harness room. I made the same excuse, to hitch up my petticoat and stockings. (I was wearing the blue ones, and in fact, they *were* rather stretched out. I fancy the embroidery on them, though.) I slipped quickly into the back hall. And, although it *was* stealing, I took the ledger. I was dreadfully put to it, to conceal it behind me all the time when I came out. It was tied around my waist with only the sash of my pinafore, and ready to slide loose at any moment!

I don't mean to be unkind, but it almost seemed good fortune for me that Lehzen has had the bad luck to have a sniffling cold this week. She was preoccupied with her nose in her handkerchief on the way back home, and so I managed to fetch in my stolen treasure. I repent *sincerely* at the bitter knowledge that I have broken a Commandment – still, I trust I have done no other person harm by so doing.

Later

I had to hide my little journal, as Lehzen came into the room, looking for her pincushion. I stuck my book and my pen under the tapestry footstool.

The reason I hid this ledger is that I do not wish *anyone* to know that it exists. Really, I must have a place to pour out my curious thoughts privately and sort through them. I never get to be truly alone. Mamma says it would be quite unsafe for a maiden princess to be unguarded by her ladies. So, someone is always nearby – across the room, just out in the hall, in the anteroom. It is not enough that I must sleep in Mamma's bedchamber: I am the only person I know who is not permitted to walk down a flight of steps without holding someone's hand.

Yet sometimes when I am sitting at the window reading or, as now, writing quietly, it is almost as if I am as alone and peaceful as a deer in the forest.

I could be perfectly happy thus, for hours at a time, perhaps, if it were not for the way Certain Persons have of *spying* on me! I suffer greatly from Their lack of trust. (And now, I fear, my feelings have driven me actually to act against my own conscience – I mean, taking this old ledger in order to defy Their wishes. Though this is a journal, not a letter. They didn't forbid me to write a journal. In fact, They didn't forbid me to write letters, only my *own* opinions in my letters.)

Of course, if anyone were to give me a pretty little leather-bound journal like the one Mamma's own brother Uncle Leopold keeps, it would only end up being used as a copybook They could read whenever They chose, and then make impertinent remarks. Although I am a princess, His Majesty King George IV's niece Victoria, I am treated this way – with Remarks – too often.

I considered that I might go into the little shop where my art tutor, Mr Westall, stopped the carriage to buy us lemon squashes to drink that hot day we went out landscape sketching. I might in that way manage to purchase one of the little memorandum books – so charming, with a little pencil attached. But They would know I'd done it, as soon as Captain Conroy made me account for what I'd spent. (Why *he* must be Mamma's financial advisor and confidential secretary, I do not know!) I'd either be scolded for spending the money, or *spied on* as to anything I wrote, or *both*.

How do I know this is so? Because Mamma herself took the letter I was writing yesterday to my darling sister, Feodora. She took it away from that bully, Captain Conroy, at least.

In the process of doing so, she behaved every inch the Duchess of Kent and Princess of Saxe-Coburg and Saalfeld.

But then she ripped it up and tossed it onto the fire! Which was, of course, burning low for economy's sake. So I had to watch the pages slowly blacken and shrivel. And I had not made a fair copy of it yet, so it was the only one! I had made it quite an interesting letter, too, for Feo, and I regret that I shan't be able to recall all the remarks as I worded them there. I was in a witty mood when I wrote them, not glum as I am now. I am *so* vexed!

"These things you write about us and our System here at Kensington are unbecoming and unkind," is all Mamma said at first.

Victoire Conroy, that traitorous, cowardly snip, the tale-carrier, was so *horridly* goody-good just then, saying, "I thought it for your safety to tell, Your Highness. Papa says you could be Prey to Others' Interests." Fine words, from someone who reads what one is writing over one's shoulder!

Toire would do or say anything to get her father to think more about her than about me. And I heartily wish he would. *He* is *not my father*, he is not even in my family. He is only my dear, dead Papa's equerry, his personal officer – a servant, if one thinks about it. But he is a military man, and Mamma admires the way he orders things. And I am to be persuaded that Their concern for me makes it all right for him to raise his voice and make himself frightful, hammering his fist on the rickety old side table with the twisted barley-sugar-stick legs. He pretends he is angry at my supposed enemies, my "rivals" for His Majesty's favour – mostly my own Uncles! – but I feel as though he is angry at me and at Mamma.

"Your wicked Uncle Ernest would be grateful to be able to show this to the King!" he accused me. Oh, he was quite beyond his usual, inattentive *Oh, hmm, oh, hmm, out of the question!* level of temper. Quite! He thundered! "He and the Tories would use it against those of us who have *only your interests* at heart!" The Tories are the political party for old-fashioned Royal rights, and nothing modern.

And Mamma said, "What you put in writing, Vickelchen, can turn up in the newspapers. You do not understand the need to be … to be … *Ach, Gott in Himmel – Stille. Ruhe…*"

To which, the baleful O'Hum thundered, "English! English! Speak to her in English! If you want Parliament to ever raise your income, they *must not* think of her as German!"

Mamma still stood straight as a duchess, but her sweet voice was very meek.

"Victoria, you must understand how to keep quiet, that was the word I wanted, how to be … *restrained.*"

Child though I am, I do understand – to a degree. The Royal Family is paid for their services to the nation according to the voting of the House of Lords and the House of Commons. They pay for Mamma and me because of my

Duke Papa, but I have so many uncles and aunts and cousins, they do not pay us much. Some of my relatives own estates and treasures, and some have to borrow from their friends.

I hear the grown-up people discuss these subjects, but I suppose I am too young to know what is important. I should be seen but not heard.

But – if I can't tell even Feo my true thoughts, how can she advise me as only a sister can, and console me in my troubles as only a sister can? Hohenlohe is so far away! Why had she to marry? It is *very* VERY bad when your dear sister has gone to live in a foreign land.

I would give all the rubies in India to be able to talk to Feo right now.

I hear Grampion the footman coming.

Later

Book under plaid cushion in Fanny's dog basket, just in time. Grampion moved the footstool over by the fireplace, to put my damp boots on. When he went out, I slipped my hand underneath the dog cushion to get my book, and also found the bit of ham bone Cook gave Fanny for barking at the rat in the umbrella stand. I have been going off, distracted, and did not finish confessing why I got this book. I suppose one reason to write regularly … is so as to be certain to tell all. Some days, a great deal occurs. Other days, scarcely anything but weather, hems being let out (or getting tripped on and ripped out), and what sort of pudding was served at tea. I shall attempt to be thorough in thinking about all that happens and what I am learning. I shall have to become a v. fast writer. (For example, that is a fast way to write "very"!)

I am going to hide this diary, where no one will come across it, and I can get it without drawing attention, and write in it. The way today has proceeded, I expect I will have the most chances to write when the bedchamber is quiet and Mamma is abed, after Lehzen has lighted the night-lights and dozed off. I cannot keep it under the mattress, for Lutie or the other maids would find it when they came in to change the linen on Mamma's and my beds. For now, I will slip it behind the big, ugly mauve settee in the upstairs drawing room. No one moves the thing, even to dust, so my book is probably safe there.

When Feo comes back to England, or when I go to Hohenlohe or Coburg or Vienna as I long to, perhaps to visit Feo and her dear husband, Prince Ernest, there … to Feo, I will show this journal. Only to you, darling sister!

See, here is a list of cows' names someone wrote in the ledger:

Baby

Dolly

Polly

Pet

Winner

Tully

Nellie

Nancy

Vinia

Rose

Agnes

Vashti

2 April

It is the most unfortunate thing for a girl not to remember her own father. Dear sister, Feodora, you must know this is so. Even you, who knew your own father for a while when you were small, and then had my own Duke Papa to be, as you said, the best of stepfathers to you and Charles – you must understand what I feel, to have *no* such store of recollections.

I try to push my memory back as far as I can make it go. Sometimes, I even pray a saint or guardian spirit will bless my memory. I would like to believe it is my own remembering that provides my idea of the tall man whose face filled the sky above my little bed. He speaks toward me, in this dream-memory I have of him, and he says, *Victoire, Liebchen. Victory.* I am not sure I remember him saying, *Victoria.*

Uncle King is the one who made them call me Alexandrina Victoria, I know. My Papa didn't much like his brother George insisting my first name be in honour of Tsar Alexander – even if he is King George IV of England. Maybe Papa first called me Drina in order not to mix me up with Mamma being "Victoire," and Captain Conroy already naming his daughter for her. Do you remember, Feo? When he died, I was only eight months old. Maybe what I remember is only what Mamma and you and our brother, Charles, and Uncle Sussex have told me. I wish my Duke Papa were still here.

Later

For breakfast this morning, we had eggs and sausages, and apples and onions fried in bacon drippings, and buns as hard as the back of your head. I asked our dear old de Spaeth, "Baroness, why is the bread so hard this morning?"

She has been Mamma's lady-in-waiting for so many years, she is always at pains to be tactful. She said, "Perhaps it is because Sir John told Cook not to waste anything." I am supposed to call Captain Conroy "Sir John" nowadays, but I shan't, not in my own book.

Later, I asked my tutor, the Reverend Mr Davys, why Captain Conroy would do such a stingy thing as to deny us fresh bread. Mr Davys said, "Perhaps because it is Lent." So I didn't say anything about sausages and bacon to Mr Davys.

Toire Conroy, that sneak, hides behind curtains to listen in, and then tattles. Unless she's lying, the bread was hard because her papa said Uncle Ernest might hire a poisoner if he goes mad, as Grandfather George did, so, there was no soft bread, which might conceal vile tinctures. Victoire says Uncle Ernest murdered his servant.

I said to her, "Did you see him do it?" She said, "No, but everyone says so." I said to her, "*I* don't say so, so, it's not *everyone*, is it?" She said, "Your Highness is not *everyone*. And you are not told *everything*." I said, "I never said I am. But *you* must not talk about the Duke of Cumberland, my Papa's big brother, that way." She said, "No, no one must say what you don't like, must they, Your Highness?" But that was not my point.

She says "Your Highness" as if she is spreading treacle on toast. Treacle with ants in it.

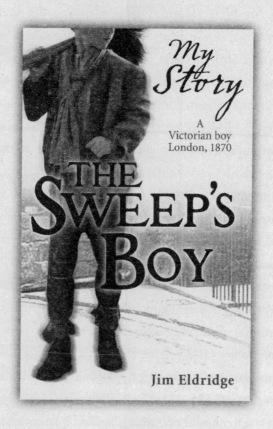

My Story

A
Victorian boy
London, 1870

THE SWEEP'S BOY

Jim Eldridge

It's 1870 when the Workhouse Master hires
Will out as a chimney sweep's boy.
It's a hard, dirty, dangerous life, and it's not long
before events take an even worse turn, as
Will's climbing skills attract the attention of the
evil Hutch, who needs just such a boy to
help him with his burglary jobs...